Ghosts of the Pacific

PHILIP ROY

RONSDALE PRESS

GHOSTS OF THE PACIFIC
Copyright © 2011 Philip Roy
Second printing April 2013

RONSDALE PRESS
3350 West 21st Avenue, Vancouver, B.C., Canada V6S 1G7
www.ronsdalepress.com

Typesetting: Julie Cochrane, in Minion 12 pt on 16
Cover Art & Design: Massive Graphic
Maps: Peter Roy
Paper: Ancient Forest Friendly "Silva" (FSC) — 100% post-consumer waste, totally chlorine-free and acid-free

Ronsdale Press wishes to thank the following for their support of its publishing program: the Canada Council for the Arts, the Government of Canada through the Canada Book Program, the British Columbia Arts Council and the Province of British Columbia through the British Columbia Book Publishing Tax Credit program.

Library and Archives Canada Cataloguing in Publication

Roy, Philip, 1960–
    Ghosts of the Pacific / Philip Roy.

(The submarine outlaw series)
ISBN 978-1-55380-130-6 (print)
ISBN 978-1-55380-136-8 (ebook) / ISBN 978-1-55380-162-7 (pdf)

    I. Title. II. Series: Roy, Philip, 1960– . Submarine outlaw series.

PS8635.O91144G56 2011   jC813'.6   C2011-903012-8

At Ronsdale Press we are committed to protecting the environment. To this end we are working with Canopy (formerly Markets Initiative) and printers to phase out our use of paper produced from ancient forests. This book is one step towards that goal.

Printed in Canada by Island Blue, B.C.

For my mother,
Ellen

ACKNOWLEDGEMENTS

I want thank the crew at Ronsdale, especially Ron, Veronica and Erinna, who patiently and tirelessly guide me towards greater structure, clarity, and coherence. I also want to thank the many young readers in schools and libraries around the country. If it was a personal fantasy that initiated this series, it is these wonderful readers who keep it going. I am so grateful for the support I receive from Thomas, Peter and Julia, whom I admire so much and learn from continually. Also my mother, Ellen, to whom this book is dedicated. She continues to be my most trusted reader and critic. I have been blessed with the greatest friends: Chris, Natasha and Chiara, whose home is my sanctuary; and many others to whom I owe thanks, including Zaan, Hugh, and Jake—a most promising young man, and sweet Dale, to whom I am more indebted than I can say. I also want to mention Diana, Maria and Sammy, Michaela, Philipp and Nini, who have inspired and supported me each in their own way.

There are people I want to acknowledge for the amazing work they are doing in their communities, such as Beth Maddigan in St. John's, Barbara Kissick in Charlottetown, Amy Schmidt in Tatamagouche, and Lisa Doucet in Halifax. These are the people who selflessly bring books to young readers across the country. It is an honour to work with them.

"The sea is dying. If the sea dies . . .
the world dies."

— NANUQ OKPIK, IGLOOLIK

"Yea, slimy things did crawl with legs
Upon the slimy sea."

— SAMUEL TAYLOR COLERIDGE,
The Rime of the Ancient Mariner

Bering
Strait

Beaufort
Sea

Bellot
Strait

King William
Island

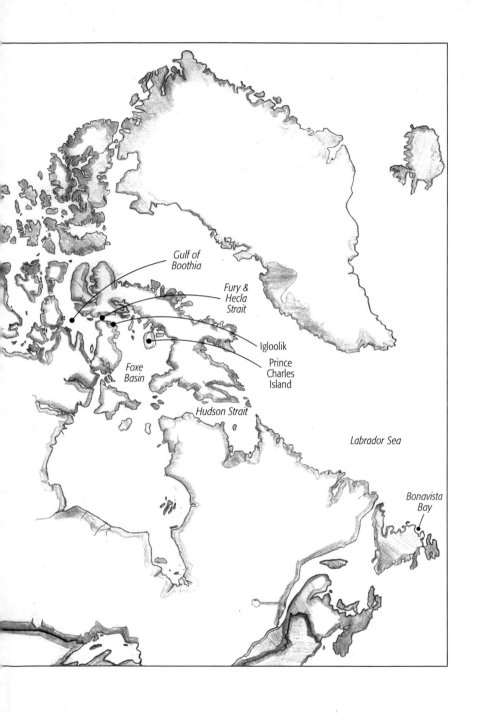

Gulf of
Boothia

Fury &
Hecla
Strait

Igloolik

Prince
Charles
Island

Foxe
Basin

Hudson Strait

Labrador Sea

Bonavista
Bay

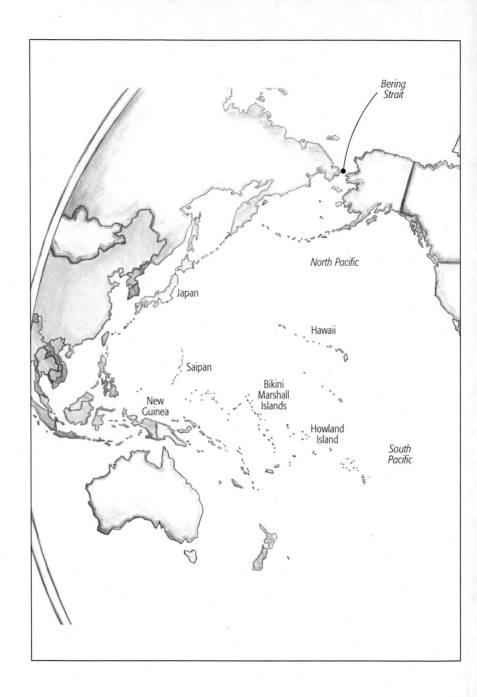

Bering
Strait

North Pacific

Japan

Hawaii

Saipan

Bikini
Marshall
Islands

New
Guinea

Howland
Island

South
Pacific

Chapter 1

I WAS FOURTEEN when I went to sea for the first time. That was two years ago. When we dragged my submarine across the sand in the middle of night and backed it into the water and unhooked it from the trailer, we didn't know if it was going to bounce up and down like a rubber duck or sink like a stone. Either way it wasn't coming out of the water. It ended up sailing perfectly, which didn't surprise me at all because it was designed by Ziegfried, a junkyard owner and genius, and my best friend, although he was more like a father to me. My own father left when my mother died, when I was born.

It took us two and a half years to build. Ziegfried was extremely fussy when he constructed things, especially things that required safety. But it was because of him that I was able to go to sea in the first place, and because of him that I am still alive two years later.

If you touched the hull of my submarine it would feel hard and cold like the shell of a loggerhead sea turtle or the fin of a whale. It is about the size of a small whale—twenty feet long and eight feet in diameter, with a portal jutting up another three feet—just big enough for one person, and a dog and seagull crew. It is beautiful in a way, swallowed up by the dark waters of Newfoundland, although it is a kind of beauty that is not really friendly. Whales don't look friendly up close; they look scary, but in a beautiful sort of way.

Inside, the sub is lined with cedar and glows with light. It is warm and cosy, even in the coldest weather and wildest storms. And though the hull is made of steel, and steel sinks like lead, the sub floats like a coconut—about three-quarters submerged. It is in perfect balance between weight and displacement. This is buoyancy. Add a little water and you sink. Add a little air and you rise. Attach an engine and propeller and you can sail anywhere in the world you want to. And you can hide. This is the magic of submarines. This is my world.

In two years we had taken three journeys: around the Maritimes, across the Atlantic and into the Mediterranean, and up the St. Lawrence River to Montreal, where I met my father and sister for the first time. Now, I wanted to go to the Pacific, a voyage that would take us right around the world. The Pacific Ocean was like a dragon in my imagination when

I was little, wrapping itself around the world and spinning typhoons and tsunamis with its tail while the rest of the world was sleeping. It is the biggest body on earth. I used to think that everything in the Pacific was bigger than everywhere else: bigger fish, bigger waves, bigger storms, bigger treasures. I still didn't know if that was true or not. And I figured it was time to find out.

But Sheba, my friend and advisor, wasn't entirely happy with my plans. Sheba was the first person I met when I went to sea the very first time. She looked like a mermaid, without the tail. She was tall, like Ziegfried, but lean and beautiful. Ziegfried fell in love with her the very first time he saw her, and he could barely speak for about two weeks after. Sheba had red hair that went all the way down to her belly, with little wave-like curls in it, and green eyes like a cat. She wore flowery, flowing dresses and jewellery that clinked and clanged every time she moved. She lived on the tiniest of islands, in Bonavista Bay, with a houseful of dogs, cats, goats, birds, reptiles, bees and butterflies. She grew all of her own food hydroponically, read for hours every day and seemed to know everything, sometimes even what was about to happen. She believed in ghosts and mermaids, and loved everybody and everything. Just being around her made you feel happy, even when her island was wrapped in fog for days on end.

Now Sheba wanted to know why, when the Pacific was filled with so many wonderful things, was I bent on seeing the darker things, the dead and ghostly things. We were sitting at her kitchen table listening to one of her mother's records. Her mother had been a famous opera singer. The music made Sheba's eyes water, even though it sounded to me like a bunch of singers trying to see who could sing the loudest. Edgar, the kitchen goat, was leaning against the wood stove and the heat was making his eyelids fall and his head droop. He had already singed his whiskers but he couldn't stay away from the stove. Sheba wrapped her hands around mine and looked searchingly into my eyes. "So. My dear young explorer, why Saipan?"

I glanced at the atlas on the table. Saipan was just a tiny speck in the vast Pacific Ocean and yet the most fascinating things had happened there—but not the kinds of things that Sheba was interested in. "Because it's so interesting. All of the things that happened there are unbelievable."

"Alfred. People died there. They died by the thousands in violent fighting. Tourists still find the skulls of soldiers in the jungle, of young men no older than you. They say the rivers ran with blood, *literally*."

"I know. I read that."

"Families jumped to their deaths from cliffs instead of surrendering."

"I know. They're called the Suicide Cliffs."

She frowned. "Alfred. They sealed up caves with people inside, or they shot flames inside and burned them alive."

I stared at Sheba's hands on mine. All of those things just made me want to go there more, but I knew she would never understand that.

"And you realize that that was where they kept the atomic bomb before they dropped it on Hiroshima, don't you?"

"Yes."

She started rubbing my hands as if she were kneading bread. "Then why on earth do you want to see all of that, you silly thing? The Pacific is a beautiful place, incredibly enormous. Why go exactly where inhumanity was let loose and ran free, creating terror?"

I shrugged. "I don't know; I just want to see those places to know that they are real. I want to see them for myself."

"Oh, they are real enough. You'll find that out. But be careful what you wish for, Alfred. We always find what we seek; we just don't always seek what we should."

"I'm always careful."

"That's not what I meant. You know what I mean."

"Yes."

"Why fill your head with the darkest side of human nature? If you invite darkness into your head, it will surely come. Why not seek things that lift you up instead, that fill your heart with joy and let you soar on the wings of happiness? Why go looking for ghosts?"

"But *you* like ghosts. You were the one who taught me not to be afraid of them."

"I like ghosts, yes, but I don't like the things that made them that way. I don't like inhumanity."

"But I want to find out if there's something about certain places that makes terrible things happen there. Or is everywhere the same? I don't think that everywhere is the same. And I already know that beautiful places exist. I've seen them."

She let go of my hands. "You're sixteen. You have to find out for yourself, I suppose."

"Exactly."

The music changed. Now there was just one woman singing and her song was very sad. Sheba's eyes welled up. I felt sad for her.

"Are you thinking of your mom?"

She looked at me with the most sympathetic gaze. "No, my dear boy, I am not. I am thinking of yours. You have no idea how much I wish she could see you now, all grown up and about to travel around the world all by yourself. She would be so proud of you. Any mother would."

"My mother would be happy to know I have a friend like you."

Sheba pulled a handkerchief from her pocket and blew her nose. "Sweet boy. Okay then, which way will you go?"

"Well, my first choice is to sail south to Bermuda, cross the Caribbean Sea and pass through the Panama Canal. That would take us to the Pacific. That's the easiest way, but I don't have papers for the sub. I'm pretty sure they'll ask me for papers if I go through the canal. If I don't have any, they could take the sub from me if they wanted to. But if I don't go through the canal, and sail around South America, it will take forever and I'd probably go insane."

"What about the Northwest Passage then, in the Arctic?"

"It's a lot shorter but it's more dangerous because of the ice. There isn't supposed to be as much ice as there used to be but it's still dangerous. Because my sub is diesel-electric it has to breathe occasionally and recharge its batteries. We can't afford to get stuck under the ice. The longest we can run the batteries underwater is twenty hours. Then we have to come up, grab air and run the engine."

"Hmmm. You have a decision to make. I will read your cards."

She got up and reached for the cards on the shelf. They were really old. They had rich, colourful, strange, magical characters on them. I thought maybe the three of us might belong there. Sheba would be a soothsayer, Ziegfried a giant, and me, the boy who goes to sea. She shuffled the cards loosely, handed them to me and told me to run my hands over them, which I did. Then she took them back, spread them across the table, turned them over one by one and began to read my future.

"*The Hanged Man*. You will turn around, Alfred. If you sail through the Panama Canal they will turn you around and force you back."

I looked at the card. The hanged man was green and had pointed shoes that curled up like fiddleheads. He was covered in leaves and hanging upside-down. "Are you sure? What about that card?"

"*The Five of Cups*." She shook her head gravely and her earrings, little Greek temples, tinkled and flashed the kitchen light over the cards. "It's worse. You will suffer loss. They will take your submarine away from you. I am sure of it."

I shook my head. I would never let that happen. "And if I sail north?"

She gathered up the cards, reshuffled them and repeated the process. "Let's see . . . *The Nine of Wands.* That's good. If you sail north you will be tested but you will triumph. Oh!"

"What?"

She clapped her hands together and burst into a smile. "*The Two of Cups.*"

"So?"

"You will find love."

"*What?*"

"You are going to find love. You will meet someone very special and feel drawn to her. Oh, Alfred, that is lovely!"

"I don't think that is lovely. I'm not going to find love. I'm an explorer. I'm sailing to the Pacific to explore, not to find love."

"Nevertheless, you will."

Chapter 2

I COULD HAVE SWORN I felt Ziegfried step onto the island in the middle of the night. I must have dreamt it; nobody was big enough to shake an island just by stepping onto it, even if he was one of the biggest men in all of Newfoundland and Sheba's island one of the tiniest. All the same, I woke with an urge to sneak outside and check. Sheba was a light sleeper. She could hear you blink in the next room. I slid my legs out of my sleeping bag without disturbing the cats on it. Hollie was sleeping on my feet and he raised his head and looked at me. I shook my head and he dropped his again. I pulled on my socks, stood up and listened. The only sound was the uneven breathing of the dogs and cats. I tiptoed into the kitchen and heard the cockatiels snoring above the stove and saw Edgar asleep in the corner by the wood box, with Marmalade the cat curled up on top of him. The night time was the only time they hung out together. I undid the latch with the tiniest sound, went out and closed the door behind me.

You had to know exactly where to step in the dark on Sheba's island or you could run into the rock or fall into the sea. I started down towards the little cove, where the sub was. There! I saw the silhouette of Ziegfried! But he didn't see me. It amazed me I had managed to get out of the house without waking Sheba. I was developing stealth. But as I stared at Ziegfried's hulking shape, not moving, I realized that Sheba was there too, swallowed up in his gigantic arms. They were hugging. I smiled. I should have known. Sheba had probably heard him in the boat when he was miles away. I turned around like a mouse and snuck back into bed.

In the morning they were sitting at the table already when I came into the kitchen. Sheba was wearing summer flowers in her hair and was beaming. Ziegfried looked as happy as a man could be, sitting next to his queen. He smelled like the sea. Edgar was leaning against his shoulder, shutting his eyes nervously every time Ziegfried reached up to scratch him.

"Al! Great to see you! I had a feeling you'd be heading north. It's a good thing I brought your parka."

I rubbed the sleep from my eyes. "I hope it's the right way to go."

"I think so. It's the shortest. It has the least traffic. And now you've been given the thumbs up."

He meant Sheba. As logical and scientific as he was, he felt deep respect for Sheba's magical knowledge. He had observed enough unexplainable phenomena to hold her in awe. He said that four hundred years ago they would have burned her at the stake for being a witch. Sheba said that they had, in another life, which was why she was more comfortable living on an isolated island off the coast of Newfoundland.

After breakfast, Ziegfried and I carried supplies from the boat to the sub. I didn't bother to pack them tightly yet; there would be lots of time to do that at sea. While we worked, we talked.

"The Northwest Passage is twenty-eight hundred miles long, Al, along the most southerly route possible. That won't bring you to the Pacific yet, just the Beaufort Sea. But from there the Pacific should be accessible enough by the end of summer. You need to allow at least a month to reach the Beaufort Sea."

"A *month*? We crossed the Atlantic in a week and a half!"

"Ice, Al. Ice is the demon waiting for you, even though they say the Arctic is freer of ice than ever before. You'll have to see that for yourself. Once you leave the Labrador Sea and wind through the passage you'll have to slow down. It isn't icebergs or sheets of ice you'll have to worry about. It's calved ice."

"Calved ice?"

"Small chunks that break off icebergs and float just beneath the surface. They're called growlers and they're pretty much invisible. The force of your impact with a growler is the mathematical square of your *speed* of impact."

"Which means . . . ?"

"Which means: if you are sailing at ten knots and you strike a growler, the force of your impact will be one hundred units. But if you are sailing twice as fast, at twenty knots, then the force of your impact will be four hundred units, *four times as much*. Get it?"

"Umm . . ."

"Imagine falling out of a tree, Al. If you climb just a bit higher, it's going to hurt twice as much when you hit the ground. Get it?"

"Got it."

Then he dropped his bushy eyebrows, stared into my eyes and spoke in his gravest tone, which reminded me of the old man in *The Rime of the Ancient Mariner*, a poem Sheba gave me to bring along on this journey. "Once you enter the ice flow, Al, sail as slowly as you can stand it. Then . . . *cut that speed in half*."

"*What*? Really?"

"Really."

"But that will take forever."

"No. It will take a month. Have you visited your grandparents yet?"

"Yup. My grandfather asked me if I was still sailing around in that old tin can."

"He did?"

"I said, yes, of course I was. He's still hoping I'll join him on his fishing boat. He sure doesn't give up easily."

"The apple doesn't fall far from the tree, Al."

"What?"

"It's an expression. It's good to be stubborn, Al. Serves you well at sea."

"Oh. My grandfather said it was a good thing I was exploring the world now because I'd be too afraid to do it when I was older. Isn't that weird?"

Ziegfried didn't answer. He just listened.

"I asked him what he meant by it and he said, 'You think you're invulnerable when you're young. Everybody does. You think nothing bad's going to happen to you. Then, when you're a little older, you realize that bad things do happen, even to you. No, you'd better get all your exploring out of your system now, Alfred, while you're still young enough.' I told him I didn't agree with that at all, that it doesn't matter how old you are. You either face your fears or you don't, it seems to me."

"That's well said, Al. What did he say to that?"

"He started talking about the weather."

Ziegfried laughed. "Sounds like your grandfather. He cares a great deal about you, Al. Make no mistake about it. That's just the way he expresses it."

"I suppose."

We sailed for the Pacific—Hollie, Seaweed and I—on the first of August, just after midnight. Ziegfried and Sheba saw us off with hugs, words of encouragement, and lots of tears.

Ziegfried and I would meet up somewhere in the Pacific, as we had done in Crete the year before. We hadn't decided where yet. As I backed the sub out of the cove, turned and headed out to sea, I stood in the portal and saluted them. They were the greatest people I would ever know. Now *my* tears fell, when no one could see them.

The sub cut through the dark like a migrating bird towards the North Pole. Hollie and I stood in the portal and let the wind blow in our faces as the bow ploughed the sea in front of us. We would sail due north for seven hundred miles before turning west into the Hudson Strait.

Ziegfried's warning to sail slowly weighed heavily on my mind. I wasn't worried about puncturing the hull if we struck ice. It was built of reinforced steel and supported by a strong wooden frame on the inside. There was also an insulating, shock-absorbing layer of rubber in between the wood and steel. Ziegfried had designed the sub to bounce like a ball if it ever struck anything. And we had struck lots of things before, including ice, and bounced well enough— sort of how you would bounce off the floor of a gymnasium if you fell. I was more concerned that a few good blows would jar things loose or crack the engine casing or break mechanical components in the drive shaft or battery set-up, not to mention the discomfort and danger to the crew being knocked around inside.

But for the first seven hundred miles we could expect ice-free sailing. And that is what we received.

It took three and a half days. We sailed on the surface with the hatch wide open and the engine cranked up, cutting eighteen knots, our fastest cruising speed, with a couple of knots of current pushing us from behind. I wished sailing was always so easy. To sleep we dove to two hundred feet, shut everything off and drifted in the deeper, slower current travelled by naval submarines and whales, either of which would have woken me with a presence on sonar.

I spent those days repacking our supplies: the canned food, boxed food and dried food that stuck out from every corner; the bananas, grapes and fresh bread that hung down from the ceiling; and the oranges, apples, potatoes and root vegetables that crowded the compartments in the stern. And I pored over the maps and charts I had of the Arctic.

The engine hummed along with a sound like perfection. Some people find the sound of waves, or the wind through trees, peaceful and soothing. For me it was the hum of our engine, even though it was, as Ziegfried called it, a "well-behaved explosion in a pretty tank." I found it comforting and reassuring. It was the sound of power and independence. It made me feel strong and confident.

We were carrying enough fuel to sail roughly ten thousand miles. That would take us to the far side of the Pacific. I would buy diesel somewhere over there to sail back. If we ever ran out of fuel I had the stationary bike, which could propel the sub at a speed of four knots when I pedalled steadily. At that rate, taking into consideration winds and currents, and how much I could pedal each day, it would probably take us about a year to reach the far side of the Pacific. But I wasn't planning on running out of fuel.

Chapter 3

ZIEGFRIED WAS AN amazing inventor. Of all his inventions, besides my sub, the one I liked the most was a doggie treadmill for Hollie. I thought it was really cool and hoped it would solve a big problem for the long distances we travelled: Hollie's need for exercise. It was two feet long and ten inches wide. It fit sideways against the inside hull, beside the stationary bike, when it wasn't being used. I simply dropped it into place whenever I pedalled, and Hollie would jump onto it immediately. The treadmill had a tiny motor with three speeds. Hollie could trot, run gently, or, if he were bursting with energy, run fast. He loved it.

He ran at the very front, leaving half of the track free.

When he wanted to get off, he ran faster and jumped off the front. The only thing we didn't anticipate was Seaweed's interest. If Hollie got something new, Seaweed wanted it too.

Seaweed would jump on after Hollie but could only stay on when the treadmill was in trot speed. Seagulls weren't built for jogging. He was twice Hollie's height but took up less space with his feet. When Seaweed was on the treadmill I had to turn my head the other way because I would start to laugh. It was the funniest thing I had ever seen. But Sheba had told me never to laugh at an animal or a bird—it was a sign of disrespect—so I had to look the other way.

Fortunately Hollie preferred a steady run, and Seaweed could only stand beside him, glare at him and occasionally nip at the track with his beak. I didn't think it was unfair; Seaweed got to fly outside for hours every day.

Another piece of new equipment was an inflatable kayak, a birthday present for me from Ziegfried and Sheba. I had tested it already and it was amazing. It was just ten feet long and cut through the water like a razor. I kept it folded beneath my seat at the panel board. That was one thing about travelling in a sub: everything had to be kept in its own exact spot and measured to the quarter inch.

The kayak inflated quickly, just like the rubber dinghy. We ran an air hose up the inside of the portal, and the kayak took only thirty seconds to inflate. I made a test to see how quickly I could pull it from under my seat, climb the portal with it, unwrap it, inflate it, grab the paddle pieces, screw them together into one, throw on a life jacket and jump into the kayak with Hollie. Two and a half minutes. We should have been on TV.

Deflating the kayak, folding it, wrapping it up and putting everything back in its place took about fifteen minutes.

The last piece of new equipment was a desalinator. It looked like a fancy teapot from ancient Persia. The metal on the bottom was thin and heated quickly, but the sides were insulated to keep the heat inside. You filled the pot with salt water and it started boiling from the bottom, creating steam, which separated the salt from the water. Steam doesn't carry salt because it's too heavy. The top of the pot was sealed except for a narrow copper tube through which the steam would escape then condense into water in another pot. But if you ran the water through only once it was still too salty to drink. Running it twice was better, though it was still a good idea to run it through a filter after that to remove the last traces of salt and other minerals, like gold. Ziegfried said that sea water carried traces of gold. The desalinator was good for cleaning rainwater too, which could be kind of salty at sea.

I discovered that first-run water from the desalinator was perfect for making stew. Sheba had shown me how to make a pot of stew in a small pressure cooker. I used one potato, one carrot, one onion, one clove of garlic, one tablespoon of butter and one pinch of spice—a mix of thyme, sage, pepper and rosemary. Ziegfried raised his eyebrows and called it "sub-stew." But if you ate it with a hard biscuit it was really good!

Seven hundred miles north of Bonavista Bay we turned sharp to the port side. The Button Islands were to the south and Resolution Island to the north as we entered the Hudson Strait. We had been sailing only three and a half days, and I couldn't believe how much the climate had already changed. The temperature had dropped from twenty-one degrees to three. The air was fresh but cold. The water looked different too, although I couldn't say why. It was just as dark at home. But here there was something else, something foreboding.

It was so hard to take Ziegfried's advice and slow down. If we didn't slow down we could sail through the Northwest Passage in a week. With Ziegfried's advice it would take a month. Could we, maybe, split the difference?

I decided to cut our speed to twelve knots. Even that was so slow I could barely stand it. I climbed the portal, strapped on the harness, stood on top of the hatch with the binoculars and scanned the water. There was no ice. And it was sunny.

Nothing showed on radar either, although my mariner's manual said not to trust radar for ice. Sometimes it will show and sometimes not. Sometimes it will leave just a shadow on the screen like the dry spot under a tree after a rain shower, except that sometimes a huge tree leaves only a small spot. Don't trust radar, they warned. Okay.

So we sailed at twelve knots, which was slower than I

wanted but faster than Ziegfried advised. Seaweed took to the air like a kite. I pedalled. Hollie ran on the treadmill. Then we stood in the portal for a few hours together and leaned against the hatch and watched the sky grow less sunny, although the sun never actually went away. It just settled behind some clouds and turned red. Then, very slowly the red faded to grey, like an element cooling down on a stove. As the sun faded, the temperature dropped. Now I was pretty sure it was freezing. It had that feel to it, as when ice forms on puddles overnight. Hollie sniffed the cold air.

"Can you smell ice, Hollie?"

He looked up. Maybe.

At the end of the day the sun was still up, glowing weakly behind darkening clouds. It was going to rain, I thought. Without darkness it was hard to know when to sleep. I steered closer to Baffin Island. We would have to drop anchor to sleep. To do that we'd have to sail close to shore. The strait was a thousand feet deep in most places.

By the time the first drops of rain fell, the cliffs of Baffin Island loomed above us. They were tall and gloomy, like silent warriors standing at the edge of the land. I bet they were beautiful in the sun. Seaweed had flown to shore. I dropped anchor in forty feet, shut the hatch, dimmed the lights, climbed into my cot and drifted off to sleep. Hollie made a reconnaissance of the sub's interior before settling on his blanket. I heard him sniffing. I knew what he was sniffing for too. I had hidden his rope.

To keep him sharp.

Nine hours later I woke, stretched, climbed the portal and opened the hatch to find a very miserable bird sitting on the hull in freezing rain. "Good morning, Seaweed. Want some breakfast?"

I fed the crew, put the kettle on for tea, poured oats into the pot for porridge and slid the bar across the inside of the portal to do chin-ups. By the time the water was boiling I had done three sets. It would have been nice to jump over the side for a swim but the water was about half of one degree. At that temperature I would be unconscious in a minute, dead in four. There's no such thing as swimming in Arctic water. Hollie would probably last a little longer than that. Seaweed could sit on the water all day.

I did have a wetsuit though. It was under the mattress on my cot. Wrapped up in the wetsuit I might last fifteen minutes or so. It was hard to say. That's what was so threatening about Arctic water: it would kill you if you fell in and didn't get out fast enough. That's why I had an unbreakable rule never to come out of the portal without the harness strapped on properly when the sub was moving. It was a matter of life and death.

After breakfast we weighed anchor and turned into the current, heading northwest. Everything was misty and rainy now, a very cold rain. Tough as he was, Seaweed must have had a nasty night. He settled down on his spot opposite Hollie and went into a deep sleep. Hollie sniffed around until he found his rope under the treadmill, carried it triumphantly to his blanket and mauled it. I climbed the portal with the binoculars, strapped on the harness and stood up for a look.

It was bleak. Visibility was poor. Should we slow down more? That's what I couldn't decide. We hadn't seen any ice yet and the water still looked clear, so I decided to stick to twelve knots. Even at that speed it would take three days just to pass through the Hudson Strait.

The next day was exactly the same—quiet and uneventful. The slow pace was really getting on my nerves. I tried to stay busy by studying charts, watching sonar, reading books and pedalling the bike. But by the morning of the third day I just had to get out of the sub, I was feeling so restless. I decided to take the kayak for a paddle.

The only safe way to do that was to wear the wetsuit. But climbing into the wetsuit was like stretching a balloon over a pop bottle. I was sweating like crazy when I finally got it all zipped up. Now, only my face was exposed, and my cheeks were squashed together like a pumpkin. A wetsuit wasn't comfortable until you dived underwater and the material became wet and lost its tightness.

I pulled the kayak from under my seat. Hollie jumped up and wagged his tail excitedly. "No, Hollie. I'm sorry. You can't come today; it's too dangerous."

He frowned. His shoulders dropped and his eyebrows fell over his eyes. Seaweed opened one eye then shut it. I felt like a mummy climbing out of a tomb trying to get up the portal with the kayak and paddles.

The wind had picked up a little bit and it blew freezing

rain into my face. I considered turning back but the wind wasn't that strong yet and I wasn't planning on going far. Besides, it had been so much work getting the suit on. So, I inflated the kayak, screwed the paddle together, shut the hatch and climbed onto the hull. I didn't bother with a life-jacket because the wetsuit was pure buoyancy. Don't be nervous, I told myself. It was just the same as getting into a kayak anywhere else. Since I had never fallen out of a boat of any kind ever, why should I worry about it now, even though I was as stiff as a board? I sat down, tied a rope around my waist and through a handle on the kayak, gave a push against the hull and was off.

The kayak was so quick. It didn't matter which way the current was flowing. It didn't matter how strong it was, or the wind; the kayak easily skimmed across the surface. This was how the Inuit used to hunt seals, in kayaks made out of sealskin. I read once that a hunter had travelled all the way from Greenland to Baffin Island in a sealskin kayak. Wow!

After a few minutes I was surprised to see the first chunk of ice. I couldn't see it clearly through the freezing rain. It was teetering on the edge of the shore next to some rocks. It was just one piece of ice all by itself. Then, oddly enough, it dropped into the water and made quite a splash. I was surprised to see how quickly the current grabbed hold of it and pulled it out. That was weird. The current wasn't *that* strong. What was going on?

Curious, I paddled towards the chunk of ice. It was mostly

submerged, just as a growler was supposed to be. I could barely see it. But it was there. It must have picked up a few rocks on shore because I saw a dark spot right at the tip of the little piece jutting up out of the water. But it was coming in my direction so quickly. How could that be? I stopped paddling for a second. I raised myself up with my hands on my thighs and tried to see more clearly. It wasn't more than a hundred feet away now. And then I saw something that made me panic: two eyes. It wasn't a chunk of ice at all—it was a polar bear!

I spun around so fast the front of the kayak came right out of the water. The polar bear chased me all the way back to the sub. It was such a strong swimmer I couldn't believe it! But I stopped panicking when I realized I could paddle faster than the bear could swim. Still, it kept coming after me and that was frightening. I couldn't make the slightest mistake, such as dropping the oar or slowing down. Polar bears eat seals and I must have looked like a seal wrapped up in my black wetsuit.

When I reached the sub I only had time to climb up, tie the kayak to a handle, open the hatch, throw the oar in and jump in. The bear was only a couple of minutes behind. I shut the hatch but couldn't leave yet because I didn't have time to deflate the kayak, and didn't want to leave it behind. I hoped the bear wouldn't rip it apart.

Inside, I caught my breath and waited. Sure enough, the bear climbed onto the hull. Man, was it ever heavy! It pulled the stern down. I ran to the periscope and turned it to look at the bear. It was huge! It was three times as big as the bears back home in Newfoundland.

I decided to dive a few feet and see if it would leave. I peeled off the wetsuit, watched and waited. The bear swam around in circles for a couple of minutes then headed towards shore. I felt kind of sorry for it now and wished I had something to give it to eat. But what do you feed a polar bear?

Once the bear was on shore I surfaced and opened the hatch. The kayak was okay. I deflated it, repacked it, hung up the wetsuit, started the engine and headed north. I wasn't feeling restless anymore.

Chapter 4

THE HUDSON STRAIT was miserable. All it did was rain. The temperature hovered around zero, sometimes a degree above, sometimes a degree below. The rain came as freezing rain and just rain. But the farther north we sailed, the lower the temperature dropped. Then the freezing rain started sticking to the sub. I kept wiping it off, but every time I came up it was back so I gave up after a while. The sub was starting to look like an igloo.

It wasn't just that it was cold, and it wasn't just that the freezing rain wouldn't stop; it was also that the farther north we went, the less darkness there was, until there was almost none. With no break from daylight I couldn't remember if it was morning, afternoon or night. I was starting to think that the Arctic could drive you crazy.

And then we hit our first chunk of ice.

It was a growler. It never showed up on radar and I never saw it from the portal. We were sailing twelve knots when we struck it dead on. It wasn't that big but it made a heck of a noise and shook everything loose that wasn't tied down. The desalinator went flying, hit the bicycle seat, spun around a few times in the air and landed just a couple of inches in front of Hollie, who saw it coming and ducked. Seaweed went up in the air with a burst of feathers. The force of impact threw me backwards and I banged my mouth against the periscope, putting a tooth through my lip. I rushed to the controls, shut off the engine, checked to see that the crew was okay and climbed the portal to take a look. In the freezing rain I couldn't see anything. But it had to be there. And I wanted to see it so I turned the engine back on, swung around and went back slowly. Sure enough, there it was, floating a couple of inches beneath the surface like a sea mine. What a menace!

We continued sailing but I reduced our speed to ten knots, climbed the portal and tried to see growlers through the freezing rain. That was pretty much impossible. We hit another one about fifteen minutes later and I never even saw it until it scraped along the starboard side. It wasn't a direct hit but it threw me sideways against the hatch. I heard commotion inside.

"You okay, Hollie?"

He appeared at the bottom of the ladder and looked up. Yup, he was okay. I knew that Seaweed would be. Seagulls have lightning-fast reflexes. They might look clumsy but they're not.

So, I dropped our speed to eight knots. That was so slow I could barely stand it, but I couldn't keep running into growlers. We struck three more before entering the Foxe Channel, but those hits weren't so bad. Ziegfried was right: dropping our speed reduced the force of impact a lot. Still, I hated hitting them, even the small ones. It was like getting hit in the head with a snowball. This was the first time I seriously considered turning around and going back. It was going to take forever to sail through the passage like this. The thought of speeding through the warmer waters of the Caribbean was so appealing. But I had to remember Sheba's warning: if I went south they would take my sub away from me. Rats. I had to keep going. To ignore Sheba's prediction would be to invite disaster.

In the Foxe Channel there were bigger chunks of ice. They were called bergy bits. They stuck out of the water like miniature icebergs and showed up on radar most of the time, though not always. But the freezing rain finally stopped and the sun began to shine. That was a huge improvement. Now I could see again. There was ice everywhere! Some of it showed on radar and some didn't. I had to watch all the time and that was exhausting! The more tired I was, the more I needed to sleep, which slowed us down even more. A bigger ship would have just pushed all of this ice out of the way.

The sun grew brighter until it became blinding. It made the ice sparkle like jewels. That was very pretty, but too bright to stare at. I had to put on sunglasses. I wished I had some for Hollie too. Whenever he was in the portal his eyes squinted into thin slits as he sniffed at the air. And sometimes he turned away, dropped his head onto my arm and shut his eyes.

At some point we crossed the Arctic Circle. I didn't know when exactly, but it sits at 66.5622 degrees latitude, and we passed that somewhere in our second week. Nothing changed much. But now we had to get out of the sub because we were going stir-crazy from being stuck inside so long.

I decided to head for Prince Charles Island since we were passing close by. My Arctic guidebook said that the island was about the size of Anticosti Island but was uninhabited. It had lots of birds. I wondered if it had lots of polar bears. Probably.

The island was flat and grey, yet it reminded me a little of North Africa, which we had seen the year before. That was weird because North Africa was hot and had gold-coloured sand and red mountains, and the Mediterranean Sea was light green and blue, and you could see through it. Prince Charles Island had a tiny bit of green mixed in with a whole bunch of grey. As we sailed closer I saw a light sprinkling of snow too. But there were no mountains or sand, and the sea was almost black. I supposed what reminded me of North Africa was that there were no telephone lines, poles, towns, farms or people. That's what North Africa had looked like to me where we first landed. Or maybe it wasn't those similarities at all, but just that that's where I was wishing we were instead.

I came in as close as possible, dropped anchor in ten feet and inflated the dinghy. We were still a hundred feet from shore, which was an important detail in case we fell out of the dinghy. It had never happened before, but here it *mustn't* happen. I couldn't be in the water for more than one minute, and the less time the better. But I was not going to spend half an hour putting on the wetsuit for such a short paddle. Besides, I couldn't run around on the beach with it on.

Hollie was so excited I had to keep him from jumping into the water and swimming to shore. Boy, would he have been in for a surprise. "No, Hollie! Sit! Stay!"

He looked at me impatiently. But he knew when I sensed danger and he imitated my caution, except for his little tail wagging like a windshield wiper on high.

We climbed into the dinghy and paddled to shore. It was cold, but not too cold, because there was no freezing rain and the wind had died. I wore my winter parka anyway as a precaution. I dropped the binoculars into one of the pockets. Seaweed was already standing on the pebbled beach looking bored. The beach was barren. Not even a scrap of food for a seagull. Seaweed wasn't impressed. But Hollie and I were. As soon as I pulled the dinghy onto the beach and slipped out of my parka we both jumped out and took off running. What a wonderful feeling!

The ground was noisy beneath our feet. There was frost between the pebbles that crunched with every step. Even Hollie's paws made crunching sounds. He ran around and around in circles as if he had never run before. Then we both ran down the beach until I was completely out of breath. I stopped. I could see my breath rising into the cold air. Everything was so quiet. I closed my eyes and listened. Except for my breathing, and Hollie's panting, there was no sound. Then, I heard the very soft sound of the wind. I opened my eyes and looked around three hundred and sixty degrees. What a bleak and barren place. It was hard to imagine this was an island the size of Anticosti Island, and there was not a single soul on it, except us.

We started back. Hollie found a stick and carried it proudly in his mouth. It was probably the only stick on the island. Growlers and bergy bits drifted by slowly in the current beside us. The ice sparkled in the sun. It showed odd colours, such as green, orange, blue and purple. Then, in the far distance I saw red. But it wasn't a sparkling red. I stopped. That wasn't ice; that was a ship.

We ran all the way back to the dinghy and I grabbed the binoculars. It was the coastguard. What would they do if they saw us? Would they keep going or investigate?

It was hard to tell if they were slowing down. They seemed

to be. Surely they wouldn't stop? More likely they would lower a small boat and investigate with that. If I saw a small boat on the water we had to skedaddle.

Sure enough, a motorized dinghy appeared at the stern of the ship. It was carrying three people in bright orange survival suits. They were coming for us.

"We have to go!" I yelled.

I grabbed Hollie, pushed the dinghy into the water and jumped in. But Hollie started to whine. He didn't want to go. I didn't blame him, but we had to. I turned to look at the approaching boat. They were zigzagging through the ice. When I turned back, Hollie was standing on the edge of the dinghy ready to jump. "Hollie! Don't!"

It was too late. He jumped out of the dinghy and starting swimming for shore, just a few feet away. I made a desperate attempt to reach him, lost my balance and fell in the water.

It was only three or four feet deep but I fell right under and became completely soaked. It was so cold! I was shocked. I stood up and looked for Hollie. He was standing at the water's edge, soaking wet. He had gone back for his stick. "Come here!" I yelled.

I went towards him. He backed up. "Come on! We have to go!"

When I stepped out of the water he came to me. I picked him up. Then I had to wade into the water up to my chest to reach the dinghy. I had been wet for at least thirty seconds already. I couldn't believe what a powerful grip the cold had and how quickly the pain spread all over my body. My skin felt as if it were burning. It was extremely painful. I reached the dinghy, put Hollie in it and climbed in. That was hard to do because my limbs were so stiff. I could not believe how quickly the cold was immobilizing me. I picked up the paddle and paddled the short distance to the sub. The coast-guard dingy was just minutes away. I saw somebody wave but couldn't wave back. I was shivering too much. I had to get inside and get warm.

I couldn't deflate the dinghy. Should I just leave it behind, I wondered? I couldn't think. I was too cold to concentrate. Get inside, I told myself. Get inside and get warm, then you will know what to do.

I pulled the dinghy rope through a handle on the portal but couldn't tie it. I got the hatch open, carried Hollie inside and shut it. I was so cold now that my hands were shaking like crazy. They would be here any second, what should I do? I couldn't dive. It was too shallow. I turned on the engine but couldn't seem to figure out which way to steer. If I moved towards shore we would get stuck on the beach. That would be a disaster. "Concentrate!" I yelled to myself.

I grabbed hold of the periscope, took a look, then put the sub in reverse. A quick peek at the sonar screen told me the bottom was now fifteen feet, now twenty, now twenty-five. I let a little water into the tanks. We didn't need to go down far. Through the periscope I saw the coastguard dinghy right outside. I was still shivering like crazy but I sat down in front of the sonar screen, turned the sub around and headed out to deeper water.

I peeled off my freezing clothes, pulled on dry ones and wrapped myself in a blanket. Hollie curled up on his blanket with his new stick and started licking his fur. I put the kettle on. A cup of hot chocolate would go a long way towards warming me up.

The coastguard ship was sailing south. I went out and stopped a quarter of a mile behind her and watched through the periscope as the motorized dinghy returned. They were towing my dinghy! Rats! I wanted it back. I was planning to go back for it after they left. Now I would have to ask them for it. Would they give it to me?

I surfaced and motored closer. I knew they couldn't catch me here. They would know that too. They would need more vessels, a helicopter or airplane and reliable sonar conditions, none of which they had. That made me more confident.

Once they saw me approaching, they turned and came towards me in their dinghy. I put my parka on. I was still shivering. I climbed the portal and opened the hatch. Seaweed spotted us, flew down and landed on the hull. "Hey, Seaweed."

The officers in the dinghy waved. This time I waved back. Then one of them spoke through a megaphone. "Are you a Canadian vessel?"

I nodded my head and yelled back. "Yes."

"Are you the Submarine Outlaw from Newfoundland?"

I nodded again. "Yes."

"Can we board your vessel and inspect it?"

"No."

They didn't like that. They didn't respond for a while. Probably they were discussing what to do next. Legally, they didn't have to ask for permission to inspect my sub because we were in Canadian waters. But they couldn't inspect us if we went underwater, and they knew that, and so they were asking politely. "We are requesting permission to inspect your vessel."

I shook my head. "Sorry."

They paused again. "It is against the law to refuse us access to inspect your vessel. Do you understand that you are breaking the law?"

"Yes."

There was a longer pause. And then: "Are you carrying weapons of any kind?"

"No."

"Are you carrying drugs or alcohol?"

"No."

"Do you want your dinghy back?"

I nodded. "Yes, please."

"We will give you back your dinghy if you will let us inspect your vessel."

I *knew* they were going to say that. Shoot! I shook my head. There was no way they were getting inside my sub. If they did they could simply say that they had changed their minds, and Hollie, Seaweed and I would be sitting in a cabin on board their ship and our exploring days would be over. I wasn't going to risk that for a rubber dinghy. "No."

They knew I meant it. Then, they did something that really surprised me. They untied the dinghy and let it drift so that I could catch it, then returned to their ship. They raised the megaphone one last time: "Be careful, Submarine Outlaw. Don't make us come searching for you."

I waved back. "I won't. Thank you!"

That was cool. I would remember them for that.

Chapter 5

THERE WAS SOMETHING on the ice. From the distance it looked like a couple of bales of hay. But I knew it could not be hay in the Arctic. Besides, it was moving. When we sailed closer it turned its head and I saw what it was. A walrus!

The walrus sat on the ice like a king surveying his kingdom. He looked like an old man with enormous tusks and giant whiskers. If he were an old man you'd think he was wise and maybe fussy.

Sheba had suggested I take pictures and sell them to magazines to pay for my voyages. This seemed like a good time to start. So, I rushed inside, cut the engine, grabbed the camera and climbed the portal. We slowed to a drift. I didn't know anything about taking pictures so I just pointed the camera and started snapping. That was easy enough. The walrus looked like he enjoyed having his picture taken.

Then I heard the sound of a small boat engine. Turning, I saw a motorboat approaching. It was carrying about a dozen people, including young kids. They were waving at me. I turned around, waved back and took their picture. Were they coming to look at the walrus? They were Inuit, probably from Igloolik, the closest community. One of the young men was wearing only a t-shirt!

They kept waving and I kept taking their picture. The closer they came, the more they waved. Then, they started to wave hysterically. Okay, that was weird. Surely they had seen lots of walruses before? Then I realized, oh, it's the submarine. They had never seen a submarine before. Now I wasn't sure what to do. Should I stay or should I go? They were friendly. I didn't want to be rude.

Suddenly the walrus jumped off the ice and disappeared. Rats! They scared him away. Now they were screaming their heads off. What the heck was wrong with them? I turned around and froze. There was a polar bear right behind me.

The bear climbed onto the hull just as I ducked inside the portal. I didn't even have time to pull the hatch down. And we couldn't dive without shutting the hatch. I couldn't flip the automatic switch either, because the bear was in the way. The motor would burn out against dead resistance.

The bear was so heavy he pulled the sub sideways. I was

afraid he was going to pull us right over. But he didn't. He stuck his nose into the portal but was too big to climb inside. I looked up. It was terrifying to see a bear so close. Hollie stood between my feet and I felt him shiver and growl but couldn't hear him over the sound of the bear's breathing. The bear sounded like a monster. Water dripped from his mouth and splashed us in the face. I could see only one of his eyes but we looked at each other. He didn't look like he was trying to eat us; he just looked curious. With my heart pounding I pointed the camera and held the button down.

The bear took a couple of sniffs, then went to the bow and pushed it down, then went to the stern and pushed it down. I shut the hatch, let a little water into the tanks, sank a few feet and watched him through the periscope. I was hoping he would move to the ice and then I could take his picture again. Now that I had finally taken the camera out, I wanted to photograph everything.

He finally swam to the ice and climbed up. He was so big! Through the periscope I saw the people in the motorboat watching him. I opened the hatch again, stuck my head out and took the bear's picture. He was sitting on the ice like a big white teddy bear. I looked at the people in the boat. The man in the t-shirt was holding a rifle. He raised it to his shoulder and aimed at the bear.

"Don't!" I yelled. "Don't!"

The bear turned and looked at the man in the boat. I

yelled at the top of my lungs. "Don't shoot him!"

The man looked at me and lowered his rifle. Now, I couldn't leave. I had to go over and talk to them. In the first place, they had saved my life. In the second, I was afraid that if I left, he would shoot the bear.

I surfaced and motored over. The little kids were still waving when our vessels touched. The older people weren't but they were smiling politely. I leaned out of the hatch. "Thank you for warning me about the bear."

"It almost killed you," said the man with the rifle.

"I know. Thank you for saving me."

"You're welcome. How come you have a submarine?"

"I'm an explorer."

"You're an explorer?"

"Yes."

"What are you exploring?"

"Well, right now I am on my way to the Pacific."

"The Pacific?"

"Yes."

"Then what are you doing here?"

"This is one of the ways you can get there from Newfoundland."

"It is?"

"Yes."

The young man bent down and spoke to the older people in the boat. Then he raised his head. "Come and have supper with us."

I followed them to Igloolik, about ten miles away. It surprised me they would travel so far through icy water in an open boat. The man with the rifle asked if he could ride inside the sub, but I explained that I had promised not to take passengers except in the case of emergency. It was too dangerous. He nodded his head then asked if he could ride on the hull. I said, no way, it was far too dangerous. Then I wondered, was he crazy?

Igloolik didn't look like much from the water. It was just a collection of flat, plain houses that appeared as if they had floated in on the tide and stayed. The land was treeless and barren. The only things that stood up were the houses. I saw about a dozen fishing boats lying on their sides on the pebbled beach. I wondered what they fished for here.

I dropped anchor in twenty feet, inflated the dinghy and paddled over with Hollie. The young man was standing at the water's edge to greet us. We shook hands and he told me his name was Stephen. Then he introduced me to everyone else, telling me their names and making sure I said hello to everyone, even the kids. But I couldn't remember a single name, except Stephen's.

They made a fuss over Hollie but told me to keep him close because of the local dogs. I picked him up right away.

The people of Igloolik were the friendliest people I had ever met. I knew right away I could trust them and didn't worry about leaving the sub alone. Stephen promised me no one would climb inside it. He took me on a tour of their houses to meet their elders. The elders were old men and women with extremely wrinkled faces, sparkling eyes and big smiles. They were so friendly I almost wondered if they thought I was a lost relative returning home. Then we went to meet the oldest man in the community. His name was Nanuq. As we walked to his house, followed by a crowd of kids, I asked Stephen why he was going to shoot the bear. He shrugged his shoulders. "Why not? Polar bears are good hunting. It was an easy shot."

"But . . . why kill it? Do you need it for food?"

"Yes. It is good to eat. But also the polar bears scare the seals away."

"Do you kill seals too?"

"Yes. Seals are very good hunting too."

"But don't you eat fish?"

"Also fish are good for eating. But fish every day is not so good."

When we reached the house, the old man was sitting at the door. He must have been watching us come. He was ancient. His skin was wrinkled like a dried potato and his hair was dry and straight like white straw. I had the feeling that people here aged twice as fast as anywhere else. I wondered if that was true.

The old man's eyes were dark and shiny, like pools of deep water. He stared at me, yet he seemed far away. I said hello. He nodded his head up and down thoughtfully, then, very slowly he said, "The sea . . . is dying."

"What?"

He took a deep breath and said it again very slowly. "The sea . . . is dying. If the sea dies, the world dies."

I looked at Stephen. He smiled.

"Why do you think the sea is dying?" I asked.

Nanuq looked out the window. Then he looked back at me. He did everything slowly. "No fish. No hares. No seals. No wolves. No bears. No whales. No caribou."

I looked at Stephen. "Is that true? Are there no fish?"

"There are some. Not like before."

Nanuq shook his head. "No fish."

"What about seals? We have lots of seals in Newfound-land."

"No seals."

"But . . . we saw a polar bear today."

"No bears."

"He means, not like before," said Stephen. "Now, the bears are like ghosts. The wolves are like ghosts. The caribou are like ghosts."

The old man seemed sure of what he was saying, but I did not want to believe him. How could I? It was the worst thing I had ever heard. How could the sea die? It couldn't. It was too big. It was too important. Maybe there were fewer whales and fish and everything else but the sea couldn't die. It just couldn't. And yet, something about the way the old man said it really bothered me. He said it softly and slowly, as if he really knew, not like he was trying to convince anyone; more as if it were a secret he had heard on the wind or from ancient spirits or something like that. I wished Sheba had heard him say it. Then she could tell me what she thought.

After visiting Nanuq, we went to a hall and sat down for a community dinner. I was served caribou meat with bannock and sweet tea. Bannock was a kind of fried bread that was really good. The tea was delicious. The caribou meat was delicious too but it kind of bothered me to eat it. I wouldn't kill a polar bear and I wouldn't kill a caribou either. But this was part of their way of life up here and they were honouring me with this meal. I didn't want to insult them by refusing to eat what they ate. And so I ate it. Hollie ate it too.

Stephen asked me how long I was staying in Igloolik. A month? I almost choked on my bread. I apologized and said that I couldn't stay at all. I had to sail through the Arctic before the ice came together again. This he understood. I was glad. Then I asked him if he knew how far the ice reached across the Arctic. He said the ice would be there until I reached open water. I asked him how far that was. He said far.

After supper we walked back to the sub. I let Stephen climb inside and look around. I figured that was okay because we never submerged or moved. We shook hands again and I thanked him for the visit. He told me I was welcome to stay with them any time and that I should stop by on my way back from the Pacific. As we sailed away, I saw him and a few others climb into their boat. They were carrying their rifles.

Chapter 6

NAVIGATING THE FURY and Hecla Strait was the first time I ever actually felt trapped in my submarine. Had I known what we were in for ahead of time, I might have turned back.

The strait was impassable to regular ships year-round because the ice never cleared. Never. An icebreaker was required to get through. Arctic ice was older and thicker than Antarctic ice because it was surrounded by land and didn't have warmer summer currents passing through to allow a melt between winters. Old ice met with new ice and grew thicker. There was supposed to be less ice than before but I wouldn't know; this was my first time in the Arctic.

Fury and *Hecla* were two ships of William Parry, the explorer who had tried to find a way through the Arctic in

1822, but failed. He wintered in Igloolik. He probably met Stephen and Nanuq's ancestors. Cool. Parry tried but couldn't get through the strait so he named it after his ships. That seemed like a good name for it because of the fury of the ice.

The strait was a hundred miles long, fifteen miles wide and three hundred feet deep in the eastern mouth. The ice was five to ten feet thick. That's what the books said and that's what I saw. All we had to do was submerge beneath the ice, motor through the strait, which would take about ten hours, and surface on the other side. That sounded easy enough. There was just one problem: I didn't know if the other side was ice-free or not. What if it wasn't and we couldn't find any place to surface? Then we'd have to motor back. But we could sail on battery power only for twenty hours. Once we ran out of power I'd have to pedal, and that was really slow. And, except for sonar, we were blind underwater. But we couldn't fully trust sonar because of the ice. I couldn't even know for sure if we were sailing in the right direction. I had read that whales had the same problem. They got trapped under the ice and drowned. That was awful.

A voice inside told me not to do it. It was too dangerous. But the only other way through the Arctic was to sail all the way back through the Hudson Strait, then north around Baffin Island into Lancaster Sound, which was the same distance as sailing to Nova Scotia. And Lancaster Sound might be ice-blocked too. It was another three hundred and fifty miles due north.

If we were facing a solid wall of ice ten feet thick I might have turned around. But we weren't. There were patches of open water. When I stood up on the portal with the binoculars and scanned the ice ahead of us, it looked like a white and grey swamp with sharp ridges, and small patches here and there that looked like quicksand holes. If we could just find a few of those holes along our way we could surface, run the engine and recharge the batteries. That would be great. We just had to find them.

I decided to try a two-mile stretch first. If that seemed too difficult, I wouldn't go any further.

I submerged to a hundred feet, set our speed at ten knots and sat down at the sonar panel with a notepad and pencil. I didn't have charts for the strait, but sonar gave a decent outline of the floor and I traced it with a pencil on paper, even though I knew this was a very imperfect kind of tracking. If we retraced our steps just a couple of miles north or south of this route the topography might look entirely different. Still, it gave me *some* kind of information and made me feel less blind.

Ten minutes later, when we should have been about two miles in, I started to surface very slowly. I was expecting to strike ice with the portal and didn't want to strike it hard. At about seven feet from the surface I heard a gentle crunch above us and we came to a stop. It didn't bother me; that's what I expected. I looked at the sonar screen but all I saw was a confusing mix of lines and shadows, none of which I could trust. I had to search for ice holes like a seal, except that I couldn't see the light shining down the way seals could because the observation window was on the bottom of the bow.

I submerged to twenty feet, pedalled a short distance, came up again and struck ice gently at six feet. After two more tries the sub came right up and we surfaced. I peeked through the periscope for polar bears before opening the hatch and sticking my head out. What a strange world this was, this sea of ice. It was how I imagined a colder planet would look: caked in ice, like a scaly, frozen skin, billions of years old.

Submerging again, I decided to try a ten-mile stretch. Feeling confident we wouldn't strike ice at a hundred feet beneath the surface, I increased our speed to twelve knots, sat down at the sonar screen and traced the topography again. Forty-five minutes later we surfaced. This time we struck ice at eight feet from the surface. On our second try we were only three feet from the surface and I heard a loud crack above. Maybe we could have pushed through but I didn't want to risk getting stuck. After four more tries I started to feel discouraged. But turning back was not a decision I could make lightly. So, I kept trying. After three more tries we broke through a thin sheet of ice and surfaced completely. It had taken nine tries this time. Yikes. But at least I could run the engine now and recharge the batteries. And we only had eighty-five miles to go.

We continued sailing. Every forty-five minutes we came

up and I searched for holes in the ice. It usually took about six tries. There were enough holes around if I just kept trying. But it was really tiring and I couldn't wait to get through the strait. I sure wouldn't want to sail through the whole Arctic this way.

When we were halfway through, Seaweed decided he wanted out, so we stayed on the surface for a few hours. I was inside cutting up vegetables for stew and Hollie was chewing the stub of a carrot when Seaweed came flying through the portal so fast he scared the heck out of us.

"Seaweed! What's going on?"

He was breathing hard and looked upset. That was weird. I looked him over but he seemed okay. I climbed the portal and stuck my head outside. I didn't see anything. Then, just fifty feet away, perched on top of a jagged bergy bit, like a silent, ghostly warrior, was a huge snowy owl. It must have chased Seaweed back to the sub. It was beautiful. I grabbed my camera. The owl stared at me while I took its picture. My Arctic guidebook said that snowy owls had been known to chase wolves away. Wow. Seaweed was lucky he had made it back to the sub in one piece. The Arctic was a dangerous place for all of us.

Our next attempt was not successful after six tries so I decided to keep going. I felt confident we could find breathing holes if we just searched long enough. I climbed up on the bike for a pedal. Hollie hopped onto the treadmill. We listened to a recording of African music that Sheba had given me. It was peaceful and soothing and helped keep us calm.

Forty-five minutes later I tried to surface again. I kept striking ice six to ten feet from the surface. After four tries I felt really frustrated. This was insane. I decided to try one last time. We struck ice at twelve feet, then the ice shifted and we rose several more feet, but not quite to the surface. As we went up I heard the ice scrape against the hull. It was a tight squeeze. Then, we stopped. I knew we were just a few feet from the surface, which meant that the top of the portal was either just above or just below the surface because it rose three feet above the hull. I pumped more air into the tanks but we didn't rise any further. Shoot! Oh, well, then I figured we'd go back down. I let water into the tanks but nothing happened. That was strange. I filled the tanks for a steep dive. Nothing happened. We were stuck!

Chapter 7

THE ICE FORMED A cocoon around us. I went to the observation window and looked down. Dark, chunky ice pressed against the window. I flicked on the floodlights but they were blocked by ice. I tried raising the periscope but it was blocked by ice. Don't panic, I told myself. There's no need to panic, just think it through.

If only I knew how far the top of the hatch was from the surface. Maybe it was above; maybe below. If it was below and I opened it, freezing water would flood in. But I could shut it. I'd get soaked and frozen but I could dry off and warm up. At least then I would know. Besides, what else could I do? If we just sat there the ice would thicken and seal us in for days, weeks, or maybe forever.

So, I climbed the ladder, took a few deep breaths and braced myself. I was going to unseal the hatch, push it up a tiny bit, hold on to it with both hands and be ready to pull it back down. I could push against the wall with my feet if I had to. I had done that before.

One, two, three . . . I opened the hatch just a crack. A drop of water hit me in the face, then a splash. I braced myself for a flood.

But it never came. Instead, I saw blinding sunlight. I lifted the hatch wide open. Another splash hit me in the face. I stuck my head out. The top of the portal was exactly level with the surface. It was like sticking your head up when you were swimming, except that I was dry. Suddenly I remembered I had filled the tanks with water. If the ice released us we would sink fast. I rushed back inside and pumped air into the tanks. We rose a few more inches, stopped, then a few more. Then the ice squeezed together beneath the hull and pushed us right up. Yes! We were on the surface now.

The sea moaned and groaned all around us. Chunks of ice were rising over other chunks and others were being pushed down. There were bergy bits sticking up like wisdom teeth with deeper roots. Nowhere was there flat ice. Everything was in movement too—a very slow movement, except for the smaller pieces falling off bigger pieces, and chunks suddenly appearing and disappearing.

I went inside for the binoculars, strapped on the harness and stood up on the hatch. As far as I could see, the ice sparkled and reflected every imaginable colour, though mostly grey and blue because of the shadows. I couldn't see the horizon. I couldn't see land. I couldn't see anything but ice stretching out endlessly. And we were stuck in the middle of it.

This was not ice you could walk on. It was like a rocky beach, except the rocks were not smooth and round; they were sharp and jagged, and there were holes where you might disappear and freeze to death in minutes. We had to stay where we were and wait for the ice to shift again and free us. I wondered how long that would be.

A long time.

Seaweed climbed the ladder, looked around very carefully, then came back down. I was glad. I didn't want him to get eaten by a snowy owl. Hollie climbed the portal with me, took a few sniffs and looked around, then wanted back down. He didn't care for the blinding sunlight. He was happy to return to his cosy blanket and continue mauling his rope.

I ran the engine and recharged the batteries but didn't put the motor in gear. I knew I had to keep the propeller free of ice build-up, but didn't know what might be in the way already, and didn't want to spin it against resistance. Instead, I spun it gently by turning the bicycle pedals. Although that was enough to keep it clear, I figured I'd have to do it every hour or so.

But that wasn't enough. Each time I turned the pedals I

felt more resistance. After a few hours they wouldn't turn at all. Now, even if we could dive, we couldn't sail. If there was ice around the propeller, how would it ever melt in this water? It wouldn't. So, I would have to go out and clear it. To do that, I'd have to put on the wetsuit. Rats.

It wasn't as though I had anything else to do. We were getting more deeply frozen in the ice all the time and the hours were starting to drag on. But since it wasn't getting dark it was hard to remember how long we were here.

I pulled on the suit, put the harness on over that, tied it to a twenty-foot length of rope and tied that to the hatch. I went out on the hull with the gaff and shut the hatch. The hull was so slippery I had to crawl to the stern on my hands and knees. I reached down and jabbed at the ice with the gaff until the propeller was free. It was hard work. Then I went back inside and took off the suit. That was a lot of work too, getting in and out of the suit. I decided to do it only every two hours; that ought to be enough. But what about sleeping? What would I do then? And what if the ice opened up while I was asleep and we missed our chance to escape?

I decided I had to stay awake.

Well, I tried. It was easier to stay awake when we were sailing. Sitting still like this, with nothing happening and nothing changing, was the most boring thing in the whole world and I couldn't stay awake. I tried everything: I made tea, rode the bike, did chin-ups, read books, checked equipment, but the moment I sat still, I started to fall asleep. So, I decided to go to bed and set my alarm for two hours. Every two hours I'd get up, put on the wetsuit, go out and clear the ice.

The first two hours felt as though I had slept for days, except that I didn't feel rested at all. It just felt like a lot of time had passed when it hadn't. I woke even more tired. I hated putting on the suit and considered going out without it, but knew I couldn't do that.

After the second two hours I felt kind of sick. I was really hoping to find that conditions had changed and we were free. We weren't. The ice was harder to clear and I felt deeply frustrated.

The third time I climbed out of the portal I felt like a zombie. I slipped on the hull, fell over the side and hit the ice hard. That hurt a lot and a jagged piece of ice cut my wetsuit at the shoulder. It was like hitting concrete. I couldn't imagine this ice ever clearing. What were we going to do?

After what seemed like forever, a day passed. We were still stuck in the ice like a frozen fish. I knew a day had passed only by watching the clock. I had stopped going out to clear ice from the propeller. I figured if we ever got free, I'd just rush out and do it all at once. It would be hard to do but I'd have a lot of energy because I'd be so excited to get the heck out of here.

One day turned into two. Never before in my life had I watched time pass so slowly. It felt like we were shipwrecked on an island. Seaweed was afraid to go out because of the snowy owl. He just hung around on the hull and slept. Hollie didn't feel like running on the treadmill and I didn't feel like pedalling. Everything seemed so pointless. I didn't want to read anymore. I didn't want to do exercises. I didn't want to do anything. I just sat and twiddled my thumbs. Now I knew why people twiddled their thumbs. When there was absolutely nothing else to do, when you couldn't even sleep, you could somehow still twiddle your thumbs. You just spun one thumb around the other. Then you spun the other one. Then you changed direction from clockwise to counterclockwise. Then you picked at your nails. Then you twiddled your thumbs again. Twiddling your thumbs was probably invented to keep people from going insane.

What I didn't want to admit was that I was afraid. Ziegfried had told me that the only thing we have to fear is fear itself. He said he believed that too—even though he couldn't always practise it. He was afraid of drowning, for instance. I sensed he was also afraid of Sheba, or afraid that she wouldn't like him. But of course she did. Fear wasn't a rational thing. I already knew that. I also knew that we were good and stuck and that our situation was more serious than I wanted to admit. I should have been trying to reach Ziegfried by shortwave to let him know what was happening, but I couldn't yet. I didn't want him to worry. I could have tried to reach the coastguard and ask them to come and rescue us, but how I would have hated that, just hated it. I couldn't make that call. Not yet.

Finally, I forced myself to read. I picked up a book on the Franklin expedition. We weren't far from where the Franklin ships went missing. I read out loud so Seaweed and Hollie could hear it too.

> The most famous ships ever to sail into the Northwest Passage were the *Erebus* and *Terror*, the two ships of the fatal Franklin expedition of 1845. They sailed into the Arctic and never sailed out. All of the crew of a hundred and twenty-eight died. They sailed from England with a three-year supply of food, tools, medical supplies, and over a thousand books. After their ships became trapped in the ice, historians believe the crew went crazy from lead poisoning, from poorly canned food. They tried valiantly to escape overland but couldn't survive the harsh conditions of the Arctic. Researchers found piles of bones on King William Island over a hundred years later. Cut marks on the bones suggest the crew had practised cannibalism.

"Hey, they ate their own crew! Can you believe it?"

Hollie and Seaweed just stared at me blankly.

"They ate their own crew! Isn't that terrible?"

Hollie dropped his head and continued chewing his rope. Seaweed looked at me with an expression that seemed to say: so?

I would never eat my crew, no matter how desperate I was. I would die of starvation first. I bent down and held Hollie's furry little head in my hands. "Would you eat me if I died, Hollie, and you were starving?"

He looked up at me with devotion in his eyes. Nope. No way. He would curl up beside me, whine and die of starvation too. He was such a loyal dog.

"How about you, Seaweed? Would you . . . ?"

Absolutely! I didn't even have to finish. He glared at me with his icy seagull eyes and I knew that he would. He wouldn't wait long to do it either.

Chapter 8

ON THE THIRD DAY, I was woken by a loud noise. It echoed across the sky like thunder. There was a crack in the ice. I jumped to my feet and climbed the portal. In the distance I saw a dark spot. I grabbed the binoculars, strapped on the harness and stood tall on the hatch. About a mile away I saw an icebreaker clearing a path for a tanker. She was cutting through the ice like a chisel. The ice was breaking up around her and a crack had crept all the way over to us. I wondered: did they see us? Would they know we were here? I looked down at the hull. Nope. Not a chance. We were caked in ice. From that distance we would have looked like any other bergy bit.

The ice began to whine and shake. The sub was shifting. I hurried to put on the wetsuit, grabbed the gaff and went out with the rope and harness. I poked and jabbed as hard as I could to clear the propeller, which took a lot of work. But the ice was breaking up around us and I was excited. Finally, I freed the prop, climbed back inside and hit the dive switch. As we went down, the sides scraped tightly against the ice. Then the scraping stopped and we were free. Yippee!

We followed the tanker, which followed the icebreaker, which broke ice all the way to Boothia Bay. But it was slow: seven knots. And it was noisy. The engines of the tanker echoed underwater with a sound that I imagined a landslide would sound like: a loud roar and continuous rumbling. There was no escaping it. It wouldn't have been a problem if we were able to sail on the surface. But we couldn't. The ice rushed in to fill the open water of the tanker's wake. We would have smashed into growler after growler, and even at seven knots that was more punishment than we could bear.

So, we stayed submerged, but fell farther behind to lessen the roar of the engines. A few hours later the sound came from starboard and grew weaker. That was the only way I knew we had entered the Gulf of Boothia. The ships were heading north. I tried to surface but failed. We were too far from the tanker's wake. I turned to starboard, cranked up our speed and chased the sound of the engines. After three more tries we surfaced into the path of broken ice and spotted the tanker. The Gulf of Boothia was just as ice-locked as the

Fury and Hecla Strait. If we had not recharged the batteries on our way through the strait we would have been in trouble now. I ran the engine for twenty minutes then submerged to catch up.

It was another whole day before the ice started to break up. The farther north we sailed, the freer it flowed, which was kind of odd. Then, rather suddenly, we came upon open water. There were growlers lurking still but we were able to sail on the surface again. Seaweed took to the air. Hollie and I climbed the portal and felt the cold wind on our faces. It felt as though we had just broken out of jail.

A few hours later I was leaning against the portal, sleepily following the tanker at eight knots when I felt I was being watched. Turning around, I saw three huge dorsal fins in the water following us. It spooked me. I raised the binoculars. Killer whales!

I had never seen a real one before. They were about the same size as the sub, twenty feet or so, but they looked so powerful. They followed for a little while, which felt weird, as if we were part of a pack or something. I wondered what they thought of us. And then, I saw something I wished I had never seen.

With an unbelievable burst of speed the killer whales shot past us, all three of them. They charged ahead just like dolphins. I followed them with the binoculars. They went up, down and around growlers but kept charging until they crashed into something. That's what it looked like. I was so curious. What did they run in to? What were they doing?

A few minutes later I knew. Pools of blood came swirling through the water, as if somebody had dumped red dye into the sea. Five hundred feet to starboard the killer whales were attacking, killing and eating another whale. It was twice their size. Water splashed high into the air. The killer whales rose out of the water as if they were jumping from trampolines. They twisted round, turned sideways, backed up and charged over and over, biting chunks out of the whale. Blood darkened the water everywhere. It was awful. I wished I could have saved the whale but that was impossible. I felt so bad for it my heart was breaking. There was absolutely nothing I could do. The worst of it was that the whale's tail was still moving. It was alive. They were eating it alive. I dropped my head. I didn't want to see it anymore.

This was nature. I knew that. I kept telling myself that. And yet I felt such a sadness that I didn't want to accept it. And that sadness stayed with me for a long time.

The water seemed to come alive with the break in the ice, especially as we approached the Bellot Strait. There were more whales and there were dolphins, seals, walruses, polar bears and fish. The seafloor was rising. The shallower mouths of rivers and straits were always good feeding grounds for creatures of the sea.

The icebreaker and tanker left us behind at the Bellot Strait. They went north; we went west through the strait.

The Bellot Strait was like a washing machine. I had never seen anything like it. It was twenty-five miles long, a mile-and-a-half wide, was framed by two enormous cliffs and had a current of eight knots! It would be fun to ride through on a rubber tube, except that you'd freeze to death if you fell in.

The current changed direction like the wind, and I had to time our trip to avoid sailing against it and the ice that the wind pushed in our way. I dropped anchor outside the mouth and watched as growlers and bergy bits came spinning out in whirlpools. Then, when they stopped, and I felt the wind shift, I weighed anchor, motored out and let the current pull us through. We bumped into ice on our way but never hit anything dead-on because everything was moving in the same direction at the same time. How I wished the whole Arctic worked like that.

When we came out, we were in the Franklin Strait, and for the very first time made a southward turn. Soon we would pass King William Island, where the *Erebus* and *Terror* had been icebound and bones from Franklin's crew had been found. I was kind of excited. Could we maybe find the ships that nobody else could find?

Not a chance! I had barely picked up King William Island on radar when the growlers began to gather. Within a couple of miles we ran into heavy ice again. No wonder no one could find the Franklin ships; the Arctic was guarding them in an icy grave. You would probably need a nuclear-powered sub to find them.

As I stood in the portal and took a last look before going under the ice once more, I tried to imagine the Franklin ships sailing in here. I couldn't imagine anything on earth more impossible.

It took us two weeks to sail into the heart of the Arctic and two weeks to sail out. It was the longest, slowest, most difficult month of my life. I wasn't sure how we would return to Newfoundland from the Pacific, but it wouldn't be through the Arctic.

Chapter 9

"HELLO, ANGEL. I hope you can hear me. I never know for sure if you can, but I will read this letter to you anyway. I hope you and your mom are feeling great. Please say hi to your mom from me. Hollie and Seaweed are here and they say hello too. Hollie is sitting on my lap. Do you want to say hello to Angel, Hollie? He is sniffing at the transmitter. You probably can't hear him. Seaweed is watching. We finally came through the Northwest Passage two days ago. It was pretty tough and I'm glad it is over. We saw lots of animals that you would like: polar bears, walruses and snowy owls. We got *really* close to a polar bear. He stuck his nose inside the hatch. The Arctic is very cold but pretty. There is too much ice and you have to sail way too slowly. It drives me crazy.

"We can't wait to sail south and run around on a warm, sunny beach somewhere. We're in the Beaufort Sea now, which is full of ice too, although there's open water next to the beach for about a mile out. There are growlers though. Growlers are chunks of ice that growl at you. Just kidding. The nice thing about where we are now is that we can walk on the beach anytime we want to. That makes Hollie happy. But we have to watch out for polar bears. There are a *lot* of polar bears in the Arctic. There are communities up here too but nobody seems to care that we are passing by. Maybe they can't see us, I don't know. I think we are in Alaska now, even though I didn't see border guards or anything. I think we must be. In a couple of days we'll turn south, finally, and sail towards warmer water. That is exciting. I hope your new school year is going well. Please say hi to our father when you see him next, and tell him that I am writing him a letter, slowly, and that I will mail it to him when I am finished. I will read this letter to you two more times now in the hope that you will hear all of it. Take good care of yourself, Angel. Love from Alfred, Hollie and Seaweed."

My sister, Angel, had a shortwave receiver that we had sent to her in Montreal. She could only receive messages; she couldn't send them. We agreed that I would send her messages on Friday nights at nine o'clock her time. Reception was better at night. If it was storming on Friday I would try on Saturday or Sunday. It always felt a little weird to send messages when nobody was answering, but I knew she would be sitting at her receiver waiting for me to call. A whole bunch of other people around the world would be listening too. That's how shortwave radio works. That's why I never mentioned where we were exactly or where we were from. And that's why I never used the word "submarine."

When we rounded the northwestern corner of Alaska, we made a sharp turn to port and started sailing due south through the Bering Strait, the shallow waterway between Alaska and Russia. If there was any waterway in the world watched closely by sonar, radar and satellite, I figured it was here.

There was lots of traffic though, and that was a good thing. There were freighters offshore sailing north and south, and smaller boats hugging the shore. Those were likely fishing boats and pleasure craft. I was hoping to blend in with them and sail unnoticed, though I didn't really think the Alaskan coastguard would let an unknown submarine sneak by, not even a small one.

The smartest thing was to stay on the surface and fly the Canadian and American flags from the portal. So long as we did that we were allowed safe passage by the Law of the Sea. They could stop us and inspect us for sure, and they could demand we sail into port if they wanted to, but they'd probably only demand that if we looked suspicious. We were pretty good at not looking suspicious.

If we were going to be inspected, I'd much rather it was by the Americans than the Russians or Canadians. It was kind of ironic to be less worried about being inspected by a country other than your own. But the Canadian government would expect the sub to meet all kinds of fussy standards of construction, and be insured, and for me to have sailing papers—all things I didn't have. Another country would only want to see a valid passport. Of course it would be different if we sailed into a foreign port and actually tried to moor. Then they would want to see registration papers and everything else.

The flags flapped loudly in the wind as we sailed south, hugging the Alaskan coast. It wasn't long before a helicopter flew overhead and took a close look at us. I waved and tried to look as friendly as possible. I carried Hollie up. Half an hour later, a small coastguard vessel approached. It was a very sleek motorized dinghy. It had two engines like rockets on the back, and three men on board. They came alongside us in a very no-nonsense manner. Two of the men were holding machine guns and the other was at the wheel. He held up a megaphone and barked at us.

"Canadian vessel?"

I shouted back loudly and obediently. "Yes, sir."

"Are you planning to dock your vessel in the United States?"

"No, sir."

"Are you carrying weapons?"

"No, sir."

"Will you grant us permission to inspect your vessel?"

I nodded my head. "Yes, sir."

They motored closer. The two officers with machine guns climbed onto the sub. They were official but friendly. One of them stood on the hull with me while his partner climbed down the portal and had a look around. He was smiling when he came out. "Take a look, John."

They switched places. "Where are you heading, son?"

"To Micronesia first. Then, I'd like to sail to the South Pacific."

The other man came up. He patted Hollie on the head. "This is quite the sub you've got. Did you sail this through the north?"

"Yes, sir. Took me a whole month."

He kicked the hull with his boot. "That's pretty cool. Don't know if I'd be comfortable travelling so far in such a small boat. Anyway, it's good you're flying the flags. Are you intending to stop anywhere along the United States coast on your way?"

"No, sir. As soon as I pass through the strait I will head southwest."

"To where?"

"To Micronesia."

"Do you have enough fuel?"

"Yes, sir."

"What do you want to see in Micronesia?"

"Lots of things. I want to visit Saipan, for sure."

"Do you have a visa to visit Saipan?"

"Not yet. I guess I'll ask for one when I get there."

I hadn't even thought about it. I just figured I'd hide the sub and sneak on shore. But I wasn't about to tell him that. He raised his eyebrows. "Well you'd better plan to wait for that, from what I hear."

I nodded. "I will."

They started to climb back into their boat. "How old are you?"

"Sixteen."

He shook his head. As they revved their engines and pulled away, he pointed to the water and yelled out, "Stay on the surface!"

"I will!"

He gave me a small wave and they were gone. I waved back. We were free to continue. What a wonderful feeling.

Chapter 10

MANY DAYS HAD passed since we left the world of floating ice. Now there was a yellow cloud on the horizon. It stretched across the sky like a giant yellow snail. It felt as though I was looking down at the exotic world of the Pacific that I had always dreamed of, into a cloud that was separating the hot world from the cold.

I was.

As we sailed beneath that cloud I felt a pocket of warm air brush my face. What a remarkable feeling. I felt it in every cell of my body. After coming through the Arctic it seemed impossible that the air and sea would ever warm up again. But they did, and it was like magic. I took off my jacket.

There was a strange smell too, like the smell of something burning—what I imagined a distant forest fire or a volcano might smell like. It was very faint. But Hollie must have smelled it too because he whined to come up the ladder with me. I climbed down and carried him up. His nose was twitching like crazy. Together we leaned against the hatch and grinned as the sub cut eighteen knots through the water—sailing south.

We sailed day after day without seeing anything, not even a bird. At night the stars and planets lit up the sky so brightly it looked as if you could reach out and touch them. The Pacific was so vast it felt as though you could sink whole planets into it and nobody would ever know they were there.

But beneath the surface was a different story. There were seamounts, which were like mountains except that they were under water. They had large bases, hillsides and summits that rose surprisingly close to the surface. We could have settled on a couple of them if I had wanted to dive that deep—three hundred feet or so—but I didn't. Something about resting the sub on a mountaintop kind of spooked me. I didn't know why. It was fascinating watching the seamounts rise on sonar. From a couple of miles down they climbed and climbed until I expected to see them jump out of the water in front of us. But they never did. When a seamount broke the surface it became an island. I had always hoped to find an island nobody else had ever seen. Perhaps on this voyage we would. I would make a monument of stones and give the island a name. I had already decided what it would be: *Ziegfried Island.*

Day after day we saw nothing but water. I didn't mind. After the Arctic, the warmth was company itself. It was almost like having a friend. I didn't feel bored. Every day the temperature rose and the nights grew longer. Then one day we heard a beep on the radar.

It was a weak signal. It flashed on the screen then disappeared. That happened when something small was riding on the surface and was sometimes above water and sometimes below. Whatever this was it was moving slowly, more slowly than a ship. More like a canoe. A ship, even a sailboat, would give a steady signal on radar. I was curious so I headed straight towards it. What could be way out here in the middle of nowhere?

Nothing. There was nothing there, and the radar stopped beeping. That was strange. I stood up on the hatch and scanned the water with the binoculars. Nothing. So, we sailed away. Ten minutes later the signal came back. It was still moving. I went back.

There was definitely nothing in the water. No vessel, no garbage, nothing. But the radar was still beeping on and off. I was starting to wonder if it was broken when I saw a tiny splash in the water. I grabbed the binoculars. I saw it! It was a sea turtle.

I figured it was a loggerhead turtle, though I had never seen one before. It was pretty big, about four or five feet long, and had a hard round shell. Somebody had painted a bright orange spot on its back and attached a small electric transmitter. That's why we were picking it up on radar: someone was tracking it.

What a lonely sight it was, a sea turtle swimming all by itself way out in the middle of the Pacific Ocean. It had nowhere to stop and rest. It had no one to communicate with. I had read that sea turtles had been crossing the earth's oceans for millions of years. Wow. It looked like it too.

We liked him right away. I decided to call him Hugh. He must have thought we were a tiny island because he swam over and leaned against the hull and rested. His eyes looked sad but I knew he probably wasn't. He probably always looked that way. Hollie didn't bark at him, he just sniffed a lot and stared. Seaweed liked him because he was the only other thing to land on besides water. He hopped onto his back right away and Hugh didn't seem to mind. I wished I could have given him something to eat but I didn't know what sea turtles ate and didn't want to make him sick.

Then, he closed his eyes and went to sleep. That's what it looked like. I didn't want to disturb him so I shut off the engine and decided to make some stew. I kept coming out to check on him but he just hugged the side of the hull with his eyes closed and rested. I went back inside.

While the stew was cooking I rode the bike and Hollie ran on the treadmill. When we stopped to eat, I checked on Hugh. He was still sleeping. I carried the camera up and took his picture. He was still sleeping an hour later, so I went to bed. It was a warm, starry night and I left the hatch open and we all drifted slowly to sleep. As I listened to the waves lap against the hull I felt glad we were giving Hugh a place to rest.

In the late morning I rose and climbed the portal beneath a hot sun. Hugh was gone. I scanned the water with the binoculars but didn't see him. I checked the radar but found nothing.

I wondered where he was going. I wondered if he was lonely. Sea turtles seemed so noble to me. They swam for months alone, crossing oceans by themselves. What a strange life. And yet, as I stood in the portal, stretched and looked across the vast Pacific, I wondered if maybe we were a little bit alike.

Hugh made me think of Amelia Earhart. She had tried to fly her plane around the world in 1937 and almost made it. She went down somewhere in the Pacific. She was never found, although people on Saipan said that the Japanese picked her out of the water, brought her to Saipan, put her in jail for a while and then shot her. They thought she was a spy.

Explorers have been trying to find her plane ever since, just like they've been trying to find the Franklin ships. In the Arctic the problem was ice. In the Pacific it was vastness. If something disappeared here, I didn't see how anybody could ever find it.

I tried to imagine Earhart flying at night and not being able to see the island where she was supposed to land. She was running out of gas. That's what her last radio communication said. She would have known that nobody could come for her. But she must have still hoped somehow that somebody would. She would also have known that when she hit the water there would be sharks—*if* she survived the crash. She must have been brave. It made me glad we travelled in a submarine.

In the afternoon I was bent over the side of the hull trying to catch a fish with a line and hook when I heard a blast of air and felt a shower of water fall on me. Turning my head I got a heck of a fright. Right beside us was an enormous whale. It was diving. I grabbed hold of a handle on the portal and held on. The whale's body kept diving as if it went on forever. I couldn't believe how big it was. Then its tail came out of the water and it was as big as the sub!

The tail spread out like an enormous fan. As it slipped beneath the water, the sub rocked back and forth. I scampered inside, grabbed the camera and came back out. When the whale surfaced again I started taking pictures.

I was pretty sure it was a blue whale. Blue whales are the biggest creatures on earth, bigger than the biggest dinosaurs ever were. I was in awe. I carried Hollie up to see it and he was in awe too, especially because the whale came back and looked at us. It swam close and looked at us with one of its enormous eyes. Hollie sniffed but didn't bark. He didn't even growl. Like me, he really was in awe. And I think he liked the whale. As big as it was, and as small as he was, they had something in common. Both were very gentle. They stared at each other. They really did. Could whales and dogs communicate? How I wished I knew what they were thinking. It sure seemed like they were communicating.

We watched the whale for half an hour. It dived two more times. Each time it came back up it blew water out of its spout like a fire hydrant and we were sprayed. I began to wonder if it were spraying us on purpose. Did whales have a sense of humour? It seemed like it. I knew that smaller whales, like belugas, liked to play. Why not one-hundred-foot blue whales?

Chapter 11

THE PACIFIC WAS so vast it boggled my mind. We sailed day after day without seeing anything but water, except for when we sailed over the tops of seamounts. Seamounts formed chains too, just like mountain ranges. And they had names. We were crossing the Emperor Seamounts. It was a good name for the chain, because it was enormous. It swept in an arc all the way from the Bering Sea to Hawaii! Holy smokes! If it were above water it would probably be the largest mountain range in the world.

I was starting to notice that whenever we approached the summit of a seamount, we began to see more whales, sharks, dolphins and fish. And then, for the first time since the Bering Sea, we came upon another vessel.

She was a fishing trawler. She was pretty big for a trawler but I supposed she'd have to be to come so far out in the ocean alone. We picked her up on radar ten miles away. We could see her long before she could see us, even though she would know we were here too, by radar. Fishing trawlers usually carried sonar for finding fish, so she could probably track us if we were underwater too, when we were close enough.

I would have avoided her except that I heard something else on radar and it bothered me. It was a weak signal. It appeared and disappeared, just like before. I wondered if it was Hugh.

Fishing trawlers have a bad reputation for catching things they're not supposed to catch, such as turtles, dolphins and sharks. They get caught in the nets and drown. I couldn't sail away thinking that might happen to Hugh.

So, I sailed closer. Two miles from the trawler I submerged to periscope depth and switched to battery. If they were paying attention they would have noticed that we had disappeared from their radar. They were moving slowly, probably dragging a huge net behind them, scooping fish or shrimp or something like that. The weak signal had been moving in their direction and then it disappeared. If it was Hugh, that meant he had gone under the surface. Where?

I motored in to half a mile, then a quarter-mile. There were several men in the open stern of the boat. They were pulling the net up with powerful motorized winches. The net was wide and probably stretched a thousand feet long. As we closed the distance I could see lots of splashing on the surface inside the net. It was full. And then I saw something that really upset me. One of the men raised a rifle, aimed at the creatures inside the net and started shooting!

I was horrified. I couldn't believe what was happening. Quickly, I surfaced just a foot above the water, leaving the hull concealed, opened the hatch and scanned the net with binoculars. There were dolphins, sharks and turtles inside. The man on the boat was slaughtering them instead of letting them out. It was insane.

I had to stop him. But I didn't know what to do. In a panic I grabbed the flare gun, tried to aim it just above the trawler, and pulled the trigger. I hoped maybe I could scare them into thinking that authorities were coming to investigate, though who would ever come out here?

The flare went off with a loud bang and made a bright orange streak towards the boat, losing height on the way and narrowly missing the men in the stern. I never meant to aim it so low. They must have thought I was shooting at them. I jumped back inside and hit the dive switch. We went down to periscope depth. I motored closer, steering in an arc around the stern of the trawler, just outside of the net. I pulled the periscope down so that they couldn't see us. But I knew they could track us if they tried. I sat at the sonar screen and studied the situation.

I just wished there was some way I could free everything.

Cautiously I raised the periscope. The men in the boat were scanning the water with binoculars but not in our direction. They didn't know where we were. Probably the net was blocking us from their sonar waves. I turned the periscope towards the net and was almost certain I saw a bright orange spot on the back of a turtle. I had to free them.

I rose so that the top of the portal was awash, took a hacksaw from the tool box, carried it up the portal and opened the hatch. Seaweed climbed up behind me and flew out. I grabbed the rim of the net and started cutting as quickly as I could. If I could just cut down four feet or so, many of the trapped creatures could escape.

It was extremely frantic. It was difficult cutting to start with, but I also had to keep an eye on the men in the boat and an eye on the sharks in the net.

I wasn't fast enough. They were going to see me any second. I jumped back down, grabbed a ten-foot length of rope, climbed up, slid into the water and tied one end of the rope around the top of the net, the other end to a handle on the portal. I had to dive underwater and hold my breath to tie the rope to the net. It was such a desperate thing to do. I was hoping to pull the top of the net down with the sub and free everything. When I climbed out of the water I felt something hit my arm and spin me around. Then I heard a rifle fire. It took me a couple of seconds to realize what had happened. I looked down at my arm and saw a gash about four inches long. It was creamy white, as if somebody had just scooped the skin away. It wasn't even bleeding yet. I was stunned and confused. Had I been shot?

My instinct told me to get my head inside the portal and so I did. I heard more shots ring out. They bounced off the hull. But where was Seaweed? Then another shot rang out. I peeked out of the portal and saw Seaweed's wings fold as he fell from the sky.

They shot him. They shot Seaweed. I was horrified. Was he killed? Was there any chance he was okay? Had they maybe just brushed his wings, maybe stunned him but he was still okay? I had to go to him. I had to find him. He would be waiting for me. He would know I would come. I had to.

The wound on my arm started to ache but was nothing compared to the pain in my heart. I pulled the hatch down and sealed it, jumped inside, rushed to the controls and hit the dive switch. The sub dove a few feet then stopped. I forgot I had tied it to the net. I put the motor in gear, cranked up full battery power and pointed the nose down for a steep dive. We started to move. But it was too slow! I filled the tanks full and kept the motor on full battery power. The motor was working hard. We were moving, but very slowly. We must have pulled one corner of the net down twenty feet or so. I hoped all the turtles, dolphins and sharks were escaping. But I also hoped the rope would snap so I could rescue Seaweed.

And then, it did. The sub suddenly lunged forward and down. We went into a very steep, fast dive. I pumped some air into the tanks and brought us level at sixty feet. I was in a panic now. My arm was starting to bleed and it was getting very sore. I pulled off my t-shirt and wrapped it around the wound. It was so ugly I didn't want to look at it. I couldn't think about it now. I had to find Seaweed.

I went a short distance, maybe two hundred feet, and rose to periscope depth. Through the periscope I saw the men trying to straighten up the net. The trapped creatures were mostly gone. The men were so busy I decided to try surfacing awash again. Maybe I could find Seaweed with the binoculars.

But the sky was growing dark. As I came up and opened the hatch I felt the first drops of rain. It was going to rain hard. When I raised the binoculars I saw blood run down my arm onto my chest. I was bleeding a lot.

I scanned the boat first. The men hadn't seen me yet. I tried to see through the water around me. Nothing. I was starting to get sick to my stomach. My head was dizzy. It felt so hopeless. I tried yelling. "Seaweed! Seaweed!"

A man in the boat saw me and reached for the rifle. I ducked back inside. I had to go. This was impossible. I shut and sealed the hatch, went down a few feet and motored a few hundred feet away. Then I surfaced completely and opened the hatch. There was no way they could shoot me from such a distance in a tossing sea. I was still hoping, hoping somehow Seaweed was all right and could make it back to us.

The rain came down hard. The wind had picked up.

Clouds on the horizon were black. A bad storm was coming. The fishing trawler looked so small from the distance. She was becoming less visible in the rain. I was struggling to believe that Seaweed was still okay. My heart was breaking. I looked down at Hollie at the bottom of the ladder. The rain was splashing down on him but I could see by his face that he knew something terrible had happened.

And then I saw something that gave me hope. Through the darkening rain I thought I saw the silhouettes of three or four birds fly to shelter on top of the trawler's bridge. Maybe the seagull they shot was not Seaweed. Maybe it was another seagull. If he were still alive he would find us. I knew he would.

I jumped inside, grabbed a bag of dog biscuits and climbed the portal. I had to do everything with my left arm; my right one was too sore now. There was blood on the ladder and it was slippery. I climbed up, stuck my torso out and shook the bag in the air. The rain poured down harder. "Come on, Seaweed! Come on!"

I waited. I had never hoped for anything so much before in my life. I shook the bag again. "Come on, Seaweed!" Now I was feeling really sick and weak. I was afraid I was going to faint. I wondered how much blood I had lost. With a last look through the binoculars I saw the men in the trawler trying to collect their net. They didn't seem to care about the approaching storm. I couldn't watch anymore; I had to go inside.

I climbed down the ladder, but was so dizzy now I had to

lie down or I was going to faint. I made it to the controls and dropped to my knees. The hatch was still wide open so I reached over and put my hand on the switch. Once I pulled the switch I could dive and leave all this madness behind. But what about Seaweed? Was he even still alive, or were those just different birds on the boat?

I had to lie down. Something inside told me not to fall asleep without shutting the hatch. The sub would fill with water and swamp. I had to protect myself. I had to protect Hollie. But what about Seaweed? My eyes welled up with tears as I gripped the switch, because I had to pull it. I had to before I fell asleep.

But I couldn't. I lay down on the floor, shut my eyes and fell asleep. The last thing I felt was Hollie licking my face, but he seemed so far away.

When I woke there were about two inches of water inside the sub. The sump pumps were running full blast. The sub was tossing and pitching. Waves were splashing in through the open hatch. My arm was throbbing with pain. My head felt funny, dizzy. I was sick. I tried to raise my head but I was so weak. I was confused. Where were we? Where was Hollie? I managed to turn my head. Hollie was on my cot. So was Seaweed!

I cried with happiness. I reached up for the automatic switch, shut the hatch, then hit the dive switch. As we went down to a hundred feet I fell back down on the floor.

I had to clean and dress my wound. It didn't matter how

sick I felt, I had to do it. I rolled over and crawled on my hands and knees to the stern, where the first-aid kit was. The sump pumps were taking the water away. I felt chilled. If I could turn up the temperature I could dry everything out and warm up. I wondered how much blood I had lost. It wasn't the kind of wound that bled constantly. It was a long gaping cut on my arm. The skin and fat were just gone. It was white at first but had filled in with blood. Now there was dried blood all over my arm, chest and stomach. It looked really bad. Hollie hopped off the cot when the floor started to show again. He started licking me. He knew I was injured. I glanced at Seaweed. He looked fine. It was another seagull they had shot.

I pulled the first-aid case down to the floor and started cleaning the wound. I poured peroxide over the open cut, and it made me cry because I was so weak and it hurt. I didn't care. Then I wrapped wound dressing around it, taped it and took tablets for the pain, though I wasn't expecting them to help much. I just wanted to sleep. I crawled over to my cot. Seaweed hopped off and I pulled myself up and collapsed. I laughed and cried nervously at the same time. All I had wanted was Seaweed to come back, and he had. Then I thought of all the creatures that had escaped from the net. Was it worth getting shot in the arm? Yes, it was. Then I laughed again, cried again and went back to sleep.

Chapter 12

".... WHAT'S THE SITUATION, AL?"

"I cut my arm."

"... bad cut? Are ... okay?"

"I'm okay. But it's swollen and really sore."

"How ... happen?"

"Uhh ... I fell."

"... fell?"

"Yes."

"... bad cut?"

"It's getting swollen."

"... fell where?"

"Uhh ... down the ladder."

". . . the ladder?"

"Yes."

I didn't want to lie to Ziegfried but I didn't want to tell him I got shot either. He would worry too much, especially when there wasn't anything he could do. It had taken hours to reach him on the shortwave. There was static but I could hear him.

"How big . . . cut?"

"It's about four inches long, half an inch wide and really deep."

"Did you . . . bone?"

"I don't know. It's really sore."

"Can you open . . . hand?"

I tried to open my hand. "A little. Not much."

"And you fell . . . *ladder*?"

"Yes."

He paused. "Al?"

"Yes?"

"Tell me . . . really happened?"

"I'm okay. Really."

"Al . . ."

"It's just my arm that's hurt. I'm all right now."

"Al . . ."

"Uhh . . . I got shot."

"*Shot*?"

"Yes, but I'm okay now. Honestly. It's just really sore."

There was a really long pause. "Are you there? Ziegfried?"

"Who shot . . . Al?"

"A fisherman."

". . . fisherman?"

"I was freeing some dolphins and turtles from their net."

There was another pause. And then, ". . . want me to come?"

"No! No! Don't come. I'm fine, I really am. I just need to know what to do about my arm. I'm afraid of it getting infected. What should I do?"

"You'd better . . . tetanus . . . Al. Also . . . antibiotics. Where are you?"

"I'm in the Pacific but I'm not close to anything. I'll probably reach the Marshall Islands in a week or so."

"Find a . . . ship, Al . . . for medical . . . supplies . . . tetanus and . . . otics. Do . . . understand?"

"Yes. I understand. I will. Thank you. Say hello to Sheba and my grandparents, please."

"Will do . . . sends . . . love. Al . . . typhoon . . . careful."

"I will. I promise."

"Look . . . self, Al."

"I will. Please don't worry. Thank you."

"Call . . . tomorrow . . ."

"I'll try."

"Bye, Al."

"Bye."

I knew this was typhoon season in the Pacific. What did ships do when a typhoon came? Where did boats like that trawler go? According to my radar the trawler hadn't left the area. Were they just planning to ride out the storm? They must have known what they were doing because the trawler was old. It had spent many years on the sea. But what was their plan when a typhoon was coming? They didn't seem to be doing anything yet.

Ziegfried said I should seek medical help from a passing ship, that I needed a tetanus shot and maybe some antibiotics. Well, I knew *one* boat I wouldn't be asking. But where would I find another one out here?

I was feeling better than before. I was just really weak and felt like sleeping a lot. My arm was swollen and very sore but it was not infected, as far as I could tell. I kept it clean and tried to hold it above my heart so that the swelling would go down. I could move my fingers but couldn't open and close my hand. I didn't think the bone was broken, but maybe it was chipped. I knew that bones took longer to heal than muscles and skin.

If a typhoon was coming there was no point in trying to go anywhere. Better to let it pass. If I sailed five hundred miles in one direction the typhoon might follow me there. Besides, in a submarine you can stay beneath the storm. The only thing I needed to do was surface from time to time to recharge the batteries and grab some air. That was hard to do in a storm, but not impossible. I didn't really know what a typhoon was like.

By the time we surfaced again, ten hours later, the sea was

a different world from when we had last submerged. The swells were gigantic now, maybe the biggest ones I had ever seen. But they weren't cresting, which meant that they hadn't reached their full height yet. I was guessing the winds were blowing forty to fifty knots, which was already a storm. When the rain hit you in the face at that speed it hurt!

I didn't open the hatch fully because, with only one good arm, it might be too hard to pull it down again. I took a peek and shut it. We stayed on the surface for half an hour, ran the engine and pumped air into the pressurized tanks. It was a punishing half-hour. The waves swung us up and down and tossed us around quite a bit. Hollie and Seaweed were used to it. They hopped onto my cot, which swung freely from bungee cords, so you didn't feel the movement of the sea as much. They settled down close to each other in the centre and prepared to wait it out.

There was a vessel on radar seven miles away. It must have been the trawler. It wasn't moving. They must have planned to ride out the storm. They didn't have any choice now. Probably they would point the bow into the oncoming waves. Still, they were in for a heck of a ride. I wondered where Hugh was. What did sea turtles do during typhoons?

We went back down to one hundred feet. I fiddled around a bit, made hot chocolate, put on some music and sat down on the floor by the observation window and leaned against the wall. Hollie jumped off my cot immediately and joined me. Then Seaweed joined us. It was peaceful. I had a hard time leaving my wound alone. I kept looking at it even though it was so ugly. I wondered how bad it really was. It was going to leave a scar; that was for sure. For the rest of my life it would remind me of the fight to save those turtles, dolphins and sharks. Strange that I would care about saving sharks—they would probably eat me if they could; that was their nature. But seeing that man stand on the boat and shoot them just felt so wrong. Every molecule in my body knew it was wrong. Everything I felt about life—about what was good and bad, what was valuable and not valuable, what was worth living for and not—rose up in me at the sight of him shooting them. If I hadn't done something about it, it would have haunted me all my life. I just knew. I was glad I had done something. Now I would wear the scar and re-member.

I supposed that fisherman was really trying to kill me.

Chapter 13

I HAD HEARD OF mega-waves. They were gigantic waves at sea that few people ever saw and lived to describe. They were supposedly hundreds of feet high. That was pretty hard to believe. A hundred-foot wave was a tsunami, and that was already unbelievably high. That was as tall as three or four houses stacked on top of one another. A wave like that would hit the shore so hard it would flatten houses and tear trees right out of the ground. Were there waves two or three times bigger than that? I didn't think so. But if you were in a sail-boat and a hundred-foot wave came along I bet it would look about five hundred feet high. That's what I thought, anyway.

I changed my opinion a bit the next time we surfaced.

We were fifty feet from the surface, when something didn't feel right. I felt the sub roll the way it did in a trough. But that was impossible; we weren't even close to the surface yet. I rushed to the periscope. The sub was moving sideways. I took a quick peek. We were still underwater but the water was grey, not black. It should have been black. We were in the trough of a giant wave. We hadn't come up to the surface; the surface had come down to us.

I hit the dive switch, grabbed Hollie with my left arm, raced to my cot and threw myself onto it, holding Hollie as snugly as I could. If the wave sucked us up, it was going to roll us like a shell in the surf. It was going to be a very rough ride. Seaweed could fend for himself better because he could jump into the air.

The stern went down sharply. We were going up. I just hoped that by the time the wave threw us, the tanks would be full of water and we'd submerge before the next wave grabbed us again.

After a few seconds we levelled out. I saw a lighter grey coming through the observation window. We were riding the crest of the wave. I held on as hard as I could with my arms and legs. It was frightening. The sub rolled upside down and we started to fall. Hollie and I fell off the bed, hit the ceiling and rolled a little. That hurt! Then the sub righted and we fell back. Then it turned upside down again and rolled around and around. I couldn't hold on to Hollie. He was lucky he was so small and quick on his feet. A bigger dog would have been hurt. Seaweed was fluttering in the air the whole time, but even he was banging against the walls. Now we were diving again. I felt the next wave's trough tug at us again but it wasn't enough to pull us up. We went down quickly.

I dove to two hundred feet. I checked Hollie and Seaweed. They seemed all right. If they had bruises I couldn't see them beneath their fur and feathers anyway. I had banged my forehead, back and arms. I sat and lifted the dressing off my wound. It was bleeding again. I was sore everywhere. I decided not to attempt surfacing again for at least ten hours. I didn't know how big that wave was but I wouldn't laugh at stories of mega-waves anymore.

Ten hours later, we came up very slowly. At fifty feet I didn't feel any tug whatsoever. At twenty-five feet I felt the spinning movement of current, but that was typical in a storm. So, I rose to periscope depth but stayed ready to fill the tanks and go back down. Through the periscope I saw a dark, stormy sea. The waves were high, maybe thirty feet or so. We were tossing around a lot but wouldn't somersault. Hollie and Seaweed jumped onto the cot anyway. I sat at the controls, turned on the engine and cranked it up. I wanted to keep the batteries full. That would only take ten minutes or so; we hadn't used much power. I turned on radar and was surprised to see a vessel in the water just three miles away. The signal was appearing and disappearing but that was probably because of the waves. Or maybe it was Hugh, but I didn't think so because he would have swum far away by now.

The vessel wasn't moving. I wondered if it was the trawler. Probably. I was curious to know, and so, after we went back down to fifty feet, I motored in that direction on battery power. Quarter of a mile away I surfaced again. I picked her up on radar right away. Strangely, I also picked up something on sonar, about half a mile down and falling slowly. Something had sunk.

From quarter of a mile I couldn't see anything through the storm: no lights, nothing. I motored closer. Maybe it *was* Hugh. But what was half a mile below and drifting down? It was pretty big.

As I closed in on the signal through the storm, I caught a glimpse of a capsized lifeboat. I was pretty sure it was from the trawler. It had the same orange stripe. The trawler had sunk.

I tried to make a search of the water around the lifeboat but it was very difficult. If I'd had the use of both arms I probably would have opened the hatch and tried harder to search but I didn't. I wasn't going to risk getting swamped, especially when I didn't see any signs of life.

A strange feeling came over me. There were powers bigger than the trawler and the storm. Bigger than the sea. It wasn't something I could explain. It was just a feeling. I felt bad for the crew. They were all dead now—though it could have been us too. This was the risk all sailors took. I couldn't help but wonder: if I had not pulled their net down, would they have left the area in time and survived the typhoon? Maybe. I didn't really think so, but maybe. On the other hand, a lot more sea creatures would have died.

I knew what Sheba would have said: she would have called it karma. It was karma that the trawler had sunk, though I never really understood what she meant by that. She would also say that their ghosts would haunt the sea now. I wasn't sure about that either. All I knew was that today those fishermen had died. Someday, hopefully far, far away, my turn would come. That wasn't a good feeling, but it wasn't a bad feeling either.

The typhoon passed and took the wind and rain with it. The sun came out strong again and the sky turned blue. But the sea still rolled in large swells. They were twenty feet at least but were wide at the bottom, round and smooth. The sub rode on top of them with so little tossing and pitching it seemed almost calm. The surface lost its choppiness and became smooth and silky. It looked like silver. Each day the swells became smaller until eventually the surface spread out flat. Now, there was no wind, waves, rain, nothing but an almost eerie calm. And then, like a ghost, the fog appeared.

I had never seen fog like this before. You couldn't see it coming; it just appeared. It wasn't fog that settled and made your hands and face wet. It was lighter than that. Light passed through it, yet I couldn't see the horizon. Hollie stood in the portal with me and we could see the stern of the sub very clearly, and the water a little beyond that, but the water beyond that just seemed to disappear into nothingness. It was the strangest feeling to open the hatch and climb out. With no sounds from the sub, no sounds from the sea or sky, there was nothing but a spooky stillness that made me feel as though we were in a dream. We couldn't see, hear or feel anything. The only thing we could do was smell— that very slight smell of something burning.

And then, there was a beep on the radar. I thought of Hugh right away. But the signal was strong and not moving. It was ten miles away. I decided this time I would sneak up on whatever it was. So, I submerged to periscope depth, cranked up the batteries and motored towards the signal.

Forty-five minutes later we were close but I couldn't see anything through the periscope. Sonar told me there was a ship here, probably a freighter by the size of her. But she was just sitting there. That was weird. I surfaced but kept my hand on the dive switch, ready to go down at the first sign of danger. Ten minutes later nothing had happened so I climbed the portal and opened the hatch. The ship was right beside us but I couldn't see her. I smelled her though. Then I heard something. I thought I must have been losing my mind. It sounded like an elephant. Then, I heard a lion. Okay, I thought, now I am dreaming.

But I wasn't.

Chapter 14

THE FREIGHTER WAS DRIFTING. In the fog there was no visibility, wind or waves, only stillness. It felt as if we were floating on air. It was weird and a little creepy. And I had definitely heard an elephant and a lion.

I steered around the ship slowly and took a peek. Her rudder was damaged. She was floating all right but couldn't sail anywhere without a rudder. She smelled like a barn. There were definitely animals on board. When I got right up under the stern I saw a sign painted on a wooden plank: *Noah's Floating Circus.*

No way! A circus ship?

It was so quiet I had the feeling the ship had been abandoned, except for the animals, but probably everyone was just sleeping. It was early in the morning. Then, I heard a splash. Had something fallen overboard? No. Someone was swimming towards us. A girl came out of the water and hopped onto the hull just like a seal jumping onto a rock. She didn't even use the handles. She bounced to her feet and came right over to me.

"Bonjour . . . ? Guten tag . . . ? Hello . . . ?"

"Uhh . . . hi."

"I saw you!" she said. She stuck out her hand. "I'm Cinnamon."

I couldn't use my right hand so I stuck out my left hand and she grabbed it and squeezed my fingertips. I had Hollie in my arms. His nose was going crazy trying to sniff her. She didn't seem to notice him. "Cinnamon? Is that your name?"

"Yes. What's yours?"

"Alfred."

"Is that a pet or food?"

"What?"

"The dog. Is it your pet or are you going to eat it?"

"Are you serious?"

"It's your pet."

"He's not a pet, he's a sailor. Like me. He's my second mate."

"Does he have a name?"

"Hollie."

Hollie stretched his head over and licked Cinnamon's arm. She broke into a smile. "He's kind of cute. Better not bring him on board though. There are snakes."

"Snakes?"

"Yes. Big ones and little ones. Visible ones and invisible ones."

"Invisible snakes?"

"Well, one went missing three years ago but we know it's still on the ship. We know that because we find a skin every now and then. And it keeps getting bigger. We used to have rabbits and cats but they're all gone now. It really likes little dogs. We used to have one too. She was really sweet."

I held Hollie more tightly.

"Where are you from?"

"Canada."

"Why are you so far away from your home? And why are you in a submarine?"

"I'm exploring."

"Exploring what?"

"Lots of things. Right now I'm on my way to Saipan."

"That's our next stop! You'll like it there. Saipan is nice. They have parties on the beach. And great food. They eat dog there though, so you'd better be careful. You are bringing your dog to a dangerous part of the world."

"I'll keep an eye on him. Is this . . . are you . . . a circus?"

"Yes. We're the best circus in Micronesia. Well, we're the only one. But we're the best one."

"How?"

"How what?"

"How do you make a circus? Do you have tents and everything?"

"Of course! That's what a circus is."

"Oh. I've never been to the circus."

Her face fell. "You've never been to the circus? Ever?"

"No. But I saw one on TV. Did I hear elephants and lions on your ship?"

"Yes, you did. We have one elephant. Mindy. She's very small. And we have two lions. René and Louis. But Louis is very old and doesn't really like to perform anymore. Can I see inside your submarine?"

"I'm sorry, I can't let you."

"Why not? Is somebody else in there?"

"No."

"Then why not?"

"It's a rule I have. It's dangerous."

"Is it dangerous for you?"

"No, not really."

"Then why would it be dangerous for me?"

"I don't know; it's just a rule. I have to make sure nobody gets hurt on my sub."

"So, change it for me."

"I don't want to change it."

"Hmmf! What happened to your arm?"

"I got shot."

"You got *shot*? Who shot you?"

"Some fishermen."

"Why did they shoot you?"

"Because I was trying to free turtles and dolphins from their net."

She furrowed her brow. "Why would you do that?"

"To rescue them."

"But why did you want to rescue them? They're good to eat."

We stared into each other's eyes. We were about the same age and almost the same height. But we were from very different worlds. I was guessing she was from India, or maybe Arabia. "Is there a medical person on your ship who could give me a tetanus shot?"

"We have everything. But don't bring Hollie, unless you want him to be eaten by a snake."

"I won't."

"Okay, I'll drop the rope ladder."

She dove into the water so gracefully there were almost no ripples. And she swam away fast. "How will you climb up?" I yelled after her.

"I can climb anything!"

I didn't know how she climbed back up the ship but she dropped the rope ladder and I tied the sub to it. I left Hollie inside. Seaweed stayed on guard on the hull. Something about the circus ship spooked him. Normally he would be exploring it for food already. He must have seen something he didn't like.

It was not easy to climb the rope ladder with one arm, and that gave Cinnamon the impression I didn't know how. And that bugged me.

"Don't worry, you won't fall."

"I know I won't fall. I'm just being careful to protect my arm."

I didn't even think I needed a tetanus shot. My arm was just really weak and sore. But I had to take Ziegfried's advice.

"I've never seen anybody climb so slowly before."

"I have a broken arm!"

"I thought you said you were shot."

"I did. That's what I meant."

"Are you making it up?"

"No! Why would I make it up?"

"I don't know. I've just never seen anybody climb so slowly before. You won't fall."

"I'm trying not to hurt my arm, or it will take forever to heal."

There were three decks on the ship and they were cluttered beyond belief. There were metal and wooden boxes fitted into every nook and cranny, and lengths of rope tied to everything, no doubt to tie it all down. They had just come through the typhoon too. There were heavy burlap sacks filled with rope and canvas and all kinds of things that should have been inside the hold. It turned the gangway into a maze. I followed Cinnamon in and around the maze and thought how many great places there were for snakes to hide. I looked at every rope carefully just to make sure it wasn't a snake.

"I don't see any snakes."

"They're here. They just don't want you to see them. They smelled you before you even climbed onto the ship."

"They did?"

"Yup."

We turned a corner into an alley and suddenly everything became darker. Things above our heads looked like snakes moving to me. "Are there snakes up there?"

"Probably."

"Are they poisonous?"

"No. They're just hungry."

"How many snakes are on this ship?"

"Nobody knows. Okay, you have to bend your head to come this way. This is where Mr. Chee lives. He's the one who can fix your arm."

"Is he a doctor?"

"Mr. Chee is everything."

"Do I have to pay him?"

"You don't have to do anything you don't want to with Mr. Chee."

We climbed down a ladder from the upper deck, twisted through aisles of supplies, went up a little way, down a longer way, wound through a few more aisles and up a few steps. It was dark most of the way. I kept turning my head quickly from side to side and could have sworn I felt things dropping down my back.

"Why is all your cargo on the decks?"

"Because we need the holds for the animals and circus practice."

"Oh."

"Okay. This is where Mr. Chee lives. You have to take your sneakers off here."

"What if he's sleeping?"

"Mr. Chee never sleeps; he just meditates."

Cinnamon knocked lightly on the door and we entered a small cabin that led to a larger one. There were candles hanging here and there, giving a soft coloured light. There was incense burning that reminded me of Sheba. Sheba would have felt comfortable in this room, I thought.

"Close the door tightly behind you; Mr. Chee doesn't allow snakes in his cabin."

"I don't blame him."

Mr. Chee was sitting crossed-legged on a seat that hung from bungee cords just like my cot. If the ship tossed and pitched, his seat swung free and kept him still. He was sitting up but he looked asleep to me. Cinnamon stood in front of him and spoke very gently. "Mr. Chee?"

"Good morning, Cinnamon and friend."

We both answered, "Good morning."

"How can I help you?"

I stepped forward. "I hurt my arm and I was hoping maybe you could give me a tetanus shot."

"When you hurt your arm?"

"Umm . . . about a week ago, I guess."

"No tetanus needed. If you need tetanus, you dead already. You have pain?"

"It's very sore. It's swollen."

"You can open hand?"

"Not very well."

"Let me see."

He hopped off his seat, lit two candelabras and carried them to a carpet on the floor and sat down. "Here."

I went over and sat down. I unwrapped my bandage and showed him my arm.

"Ahhhhh . . . gunshot wound."

He looked me directly in the eye. He was old and wise. I liked him. "You are living dangerously."

I shrugged. "Sometimes, I guess."

He held my arm with both of his hands and felt it very gently. He brought it close to his face and drew his eyes over my skin like an x-ray. "When you were shot, you were thrown back, yes?"

"Yes."

"Not just cut skin. You have chipped bone and torn ligament. Very sore."

"It *is* very sore."

I looked at Cinnamon. I *told* you, I wanted to say.

"I will make pain go away, but you must let arm rest. Live less dangerous."

He smiled. Then he reached for a long box, opened it and pulled out a whole bunch of very long needles.

Chapter 15

NEEDLES WERE STICKING out of my arm, but all I felt was a curious tingling and a warm, pleasant sensation. When Mr. Chee removed the needles, the pain was gone. It was the most amazing thing. I couldn't believe it. "Thank you so much, Mr. Chee. I don't know how it works but it really works."

Mr. Chee bowed his head. "Ancient Chinese medicine. Now, you live less dangerous."

"I will. How much should I pay you?"

He looked at me and smiled. "You rich?"

"No."

"Ten dollars."

"Okay. I will go to my sub to get it."

He pointed his finger at me. "No more dangerous living."
I shrugged. Cinnamon looked suddenly worried. "Alfred."
"Yes?"
"Did you leave your sub open?"
"Yes. Why?"
"Oh my gosh!"
"Why? What's wrong?"
"I'm afraid to tell you."
"What? Tell me!"
"Snakes can swim."
I stared dumbly for a second, trying to understand what she meant. Then I burst from the room and raced through the decks of the ship like a mad man. Cinnamon came after me, shouting at me which way to go. I ran around things, jumped over things and ducked my head. I went up and down ladders with my feet barely touching the steps. When we came out on deck I raced towards the stern. Cinnamon was still yelling something to me but I couldn't listen now. I could hear Seaweed squawking in alarm. No! No! No! No! I took a quick glance over the edge of the ship and jumped.

On the way down I tried to tuck my arm in close to my body. I knew it was going to hurt a lot. And it did. But I ignored it. I swam to the sub. I heard another splash. Cinnamon was coming. The worst thing was that I couldn't hear Hollie barking. Hollie would always bark at an intruder. I climbed the hull and jumped inside. I looked around but didn't see anything. Then I saw I had left the engine compartment open. "Hollie!"

I thought I heard him whine. I rushed into the engine compartment. The snake was there, coiled around the engine. It was huge! Where was Hollie? I looked and looked but didn't see him. "Hollie?"

Now I heard him whine for sure. He had wedged himself underneath the engine in an impossible position. The snake's head was so big there wasn't enough room for it to open its mouth wide enough to grab him. It could reach him but it couldn't bite him. And it had been trying. Hollie was frightened to death.

"It's okay, Hollie. I'll get him!"

I reached for the biggest wrench. The snake started to coil more tightly. I tried to push it with my foot. I was going to strike it on the head if I could get a clear shot. It didn't like me touching it but it wouldn't leave. It didn't want to lose its prey. I raised the wrench.

"Don't!" Cinnamon screamed. "Don't hurt it!"

"Why not?"

"You don't have to hurt it. It's okay. I will take it away."

"How?"

The snake was at least twelve feet long; it was hard to tell exactly because it was coiled up. Cinnamon stood in front of me. "Please. Just back away for a moment and I will take it out."

"Okay, but if I see it go for Hollie I'm going to hit it with all my strength."

"Please don't. It's okay, he'll come with me. He's just hungry."

I stepped back but stayed ready. Cinnamon bent down close to the snake and spoke to it softly, then she reached her hand very gently towards its head. The snake turned and stuck its tongue out at her. It was smelling her. Slowly its whole body began to move. It moved all at once, almost magically. Its head began to run up Cinnamon's arm and across her shoulder.

"Are you sure you know what you're doing?"

"Shhhhh. When I start to move, very gently pick up the tail, okay, and follow me. He's really heavy. He has grown so much. Megara will be amazed."

"Who's Megara?"

"The snake lady. Okay. Can you carry his tail? Carefully. Don't make any jerky movements."

As much as I didn't like snakes, I picked up the back end and followed Cinnamon. She was wearing the rest of him like a really long scarf. Together we made our way towards the portal. I looked back at Hollie. "It's okay now, Hollie. You can come out."

Cinnamon went up the ladder first. But the snake started to leave on its own before we got to the top. It slithered down the side of the hull, across the water and up the rope ladder. I went back inside, into the engine compartment, crouched down and coaxed Hollie out. The poor thing. I reached in with both hands and helped him out. I didn't know how he got in there in the first place. It was probably the only place in the whole sub where the snake couldn't reach him.

I carried Hollie to his blanket and we sat down together.

Now I felt pain. It was twice as bad as before. I could tell that Hollie wasn't feeling so great either. I patted his fur and spoke gently to him to help calm him down. I told him what a brave and smart dog he was, and I promised to take better care of him. But Hollie knew, as I knew, that there were no guarantees. His first owner had thrown him off a wharf because he was the runt of the litter. I figured he carried few expectations in life after that: you could see it in his eyes. And yet he fought fiercely for the life that he had. I figured any other dog would have been in the belly of that snake already. I saw feet coming down the portal.

"Are you okay? I never saw anybody move so fast before. I never saw anybody jump so high from the ship without looking."

"I looked."

"It didn't look like it. How is your arm?"

It was so painful I almost couldn't speak. I shut my eyes and concentrated.

"You've got to come back to Mr. Chee, Alfred. He'll help you."

I couldn't argue with that. "You see that little room there, at the stern? Could you please go into it, open up the tool bag there and empty it on the floor, then bring the tool bag back?"

"You want the empty tool bag? Okay. Why?"

I tried to get up, and winced with the pain. "That's how I carry Hollie. He's coming with me this time."

"Are you sure you . . . ?"

"Yes. He's coming with me."

I shut and sealed the hatch behind us. I wouldn't let Hollie out of my sight. If any snakes tried to attack him while we were on the ship I would kill them. I really would. I had strapped my knife onto my belt.

Cinnamon helped me up the rope ladder. It hurt so much now it made my eyes water, though I wasn't crying. Hollie sat in the tool bag, a tough nylon mesh bag that hung over my shoulder. He had travelled in it before and was comfortable and safe.

People were waking up on the ship. I saw a man covered in hair. His face and arms were thick with dark brown hair a couple of inches long. He looked as surprised to see me as I was to see him. "Morning, Cin. Find a stowaway?"

"Good morning, Tomas. This is Alfred. He has a submarine."

"Interesting."

I reached out my left hand and he crunched my fingers. We stared at each other and I wondered if he thought I was joining the circus.

"I'm just visiting."

"He's the wolf man," Cinnamon said as we went down a ladder. "He was born that way."

"Cool."

Then we ran into a thin, quiet man who stepped out of our way to let us pass.

"Good morning, Edouard," Cinnamon said.

"Good morning."

I said good morning too, but Edouard didn't respond and didn't make eye contact with me. He seemed extremely shy.

"He's the Master of Ceremonies," Cinnamon whispered.

"The Master of Ceremonies? How can *he* be the Master of Ceremonies?"

"I don't know; he just is. You should hear him. He makes everyone super-excited."

That was hard to imagine.

"Cinny!" barked a bald man with a large, curled moustache and a big belly. "Sweep up after Mindy!"

"Yah, I will."

"That's Pierre," Cinnamon said as we went up a short ladder. "He's the strong man."

"He doesn't look that strong to me."

She stopped and whispered. "He uses magnets. Don't tell anybody."

"He uses magnets? How?"

"They're under the stage. He makes the audience try to pick the weights up first. Then he releases the magnets with a foot lever."

"That's cheating."

"No, it isn't. It's the circus."

"Why is he so angry at you anyway?"

"He's not angry; he's just like that in the morning. By evening he's nice as can be."

We reached Mr. Chee's door and Cinnamon knocked. We

took off our shoes and entered. Mr. Chee was back on his swinging chair. "Something happened. What happened? You have pain again so fast. How can you have pain again so fast?"

"I jumped off the ship to rescue my dog from a snake."

"You jump off ship?" Mr. Chee started to laugh. "You leave acupuncture and jump off ship?"

He laughed harder. He had such a funny laugh that Cinnamon and I started laughing too. But though I was laughing, Mr. Chee could tell that I was in severe pain. I had to sit down. I pulled Hollie off my shoulder and put him down. The room started to spin and I fell onto my knees.

"Okay, okay. No more laughing now. Now you sit with head between your knees like this."

Mr. Chee helped me get comfortable. "Now you breathe like this."

I imitated him. He brought some pillows over and put them behind me. "First you rest. Then, acupuncture."

A little while later I had needles sticking out of my arm, shoulder, back and head. I felt like a porcupine. But Mr. Chee had worked his magic again: the pain was gone.

Chapter 16

WE SPENT THE afternoon on the stern of the ship, dangling our feet over the side and watching for fins in the water. If you stared long enough every wave seemed to turn into a fin. The fog had disappeared. Under the hot sun we shared a fat, ripe papaya and some pineapple. Mr. Chee told me to eat lots of papaya, because it was good for damaged tissue. I should also meditate on how to live a life less dangerous, he said. I promised to try.

It was pleasant sitting with Cinnamon. She was so strong and smooth she reminded me of the sub's engine in a way. But I didn't think she would appreciate the comparison so I kept it to myself. As we dangled our feet over the side and

stuffed ourselves with sweet papaya, she told me where she
came from and why she joined the circus. Hollie lay beside
me with his head on his paws. He kept one eye closed and
one open, watching the deck.

"I was born in Goa."

"Where's that?"

"India. It's on the west coast. We were really poor. My
father worked in the fields and my mother made dresses to
sell to tourists. One day my father got bitten by a poisonous
snake. His leg swelled up really badly and he went blind.
Because my father couldn't work anymore my brother and I
started begging for money from tourists. Then one day my
brother went missing.

He was younger than me. Some kids told me they saw
him climb on a ship, so I went looking on that ship. It was
dark. I didn't find him. Before I could get off, the ship started
to move, so I hid. Then I fell asleep. I didn't get off the ship
until it reached Sri Lanka. I was so hungry and thirsty I
thought I was going to die. But I was more afraid of getting
caught. Then I saw this ship. Because it was a circus ship I
thought the people would be friendly to me, and they were.
The first person I saw was Megara. She took me into her
cabin. At first I was afraid of all the snakes, but they are not
poisonous snakes here and they are friendly. And that's how
I joined the circus."

"But didn't you want to go back home? Didn't you miss
your family?"

"Yes, at first I did. But I never knew how to get back home.

And then the circus became my home. I love the circus. I wasn't happy in India. We were always so poor. I hardly even knew my parents because they were always working, and there were so many of us. My father didn't even remember my name most of the time. The only one I miss is my brother. Every day I say a prayer for him and hope that he is all right. Someday I will find him and bring him here to be in the circus with me. That's why I save my money."

We sat quietly for a long time. "Did you ever go to school?"

"No."

"Can you read and write?"

"A little. Megara taught me. I can write my name. I help paint the signs for the circus. I can say words in seven languages."

"I hope you find your brother."

"I will. Someday."

When darkness fell, the ship came alive. The gangplanks and passageways lit up with coloured lights and people appeared from out of nowhere and seemed in a hurry to go somewhere, even though there was nowhere to go.

"Oh! I'm late. I have to practise," Cinnamon said suddenly. "Will you stay and watch?"

"Okay. Sure."

"Great. After, I will take you to meet Megara."

Hollie and I followed her to one of the holds of the ship. It was set up with hanging bars, swings, ropes and trampolines. A man and woman were there already, dressed in leotards and swinging from ropes. "You're late, Cinnamon."

"Sorry."

She disappeared into a room and came back wearing a leotard. Although she was slim, she was all muscle. Her muscles showed through her suit. I watched as she took a short run, jumped into the air, caught a rope and climbed up like a squirrel. Then, she began swinging back and forth, catching the hands of the other two. They were just warming up. They held on to ropes with their feet just as well as with their hands. It was pretty amazing. After a while they switched to the hanging swings. I was nervous at first because I didn't see how they could catch each other while they were making somersaults in the air, but they always did. The older couple were pretty good at it but there was something special about Cinnamon. It was as if she could fly. I could have watched her all day. After a few hours she suddenly dropped in front of me, sweating and out of breath. "Okay. I'm done. Let's go eat. I'm starving."

We passed through another hold, and I saw Mindy, a small, fat and very friendly elephant. We also saw the two lions. I was surprised to see that their cages were wide open. René, the young lion, roared when he saw me, and that frightened Hollie and me, but Cinnamon said not to pay any attention to him; it was just for show. "Just act a little scared." That was easy. There was also a pony with big, soft, sad eyes. Cinnamon gave her a hug and kiss. The pony seemed very interested in Hollie.

"She used to have a dog partner but . . . he's gone now."

"The snakes?"

"Yup."

I shook my head. "How do you live with snakes? That's crazy!"

"No, it isn't. It's just that certain animals go well together and certain ones don't. Just like people."

We stopped in the kitchen. It reminded me a little of Sheba's kitchen because it smelled good and there were herbs and spices everywhere. The cook was Pierre, the bald and burly strongman with the moustache. He was wearing a heavy frown when we came in, just as in the morning, but when he scooped up two bowls of soup and laid a plate of fresh bread in front of us his face burst into a warm smile.

"Thank you, Pierre."

"Thank you," I said.

He nodded thoughtfully, raised his chest, stared down his nose at Cinnamon and sighed. "You're skin and bones. I don't know how you can fly through the air on so little. Eat three bowls. Eat a loaf of bread. Put some fat on you!"

He slapped his stomach. That's where most of his muscle was, it seemed to me. Ziegfried could have picked him up and carried him over his head. But Cinnamon was right: he was a lot friendlier at night. He looked at me curiously. "Are you sailing around the world in that tin can?"

I smiled. "Pretty much, I guess."

"Well, you'd better find some place to hide before the typhoon hits."

"Typhoon? We already had the typhoon."

Pierre bellowed out a laugh. "No, that was just a storm. When the typhoon hits, you'll know what a typhoon is. It'll probably come next week. Stay away from the islands north of Saipan because they've been rumbling undersea and Megara says Anatahan's going to blow any time now. And she knows."

"Blow?"

"Volcanic eruption. If it blows undersea there'll be a tsunami. Though I suppose you're in a submarine. How deep can you dive in that thing?"

"Four hundred feet."

He nodded but looked as though he were already thinking of something else. "Have more soup."

After supper we went to Megara's cabin. It was in one corner of the ship, away from everybody else. Cinnamon knocked and opened the door.

"Should we take our shoes off?"

"No, leave them on."

I followed her in. Hollie jumped to his feet in the tool bag.

"It's okay, Hollie, it's okay. We won't stay long."

The room was bigger than a normal cabin. It was lit with soft light. Megara was standing in the centre. She was short and stocky and had white hair. At a glance, I had the impression she was what Cinnamon might look like in fifty years, except that Cinnamon was a lot prettier. Megara was wearing so many snakes I couldn't see her clothes. In the dim light I noticed something else—movement. The room was moving with snakes.

Megara opened her arms and Cinnamon went to her and they hugged.

"My darling," said Megara. "This is the young man you told me about?"

"Yes. This is Alfred. Hollie is on his back. He's a dog, but he's not a pet."

Megara's eyes lit up. "Oh? Is he food?"

"No! No, he's part of my crew."

"Is he for sale?"

"No. Definitely not."

"Would you trade him for a snake?"

"No way! No, thanks."

"Snakes make wonderful pets."

An image passed through my mind of snakes slithering all over my submarine. I felt something bump against me below the tool bag. I turned and saw a snake sniffing at Hollie. "Go away," I said.

"They're just curious," Megara said. They won't do any harm. Come, sit with me."

We went over and sat down on a plush Indian rug. I pulled Hollie from my back and put him on the floor between my legs, still in the tool bag. I wouldn't dare open the bag in here. Cinnamon sat in front of Megara, who began to brush her hair affectionately. I felt a snake touch lightly on my shoulder and I gently brushed it away.

"Snakes are curious and very friendly once they become comfortable with you."

Megara continued talking but I was struggling to pay attention. It seemed to me that all the snakes in the room were slowly making their way towards us. They came from the floor, the walls, even the ceiling. They rolled like waves over Megara's shoulders, down across her lap and over Cinnamon. Cinnamon sat silent and peaceful. She was enjoying having her hair brushed. Megara seemed to have become like a mother to her. Cinnamon's eyes began to droop. It was warm in the room. I felt drowsy too. There was something almost hypnotic about the soft light and movement of snakes. But I knew I had to stay awake and stay alert.

Cinnamon shifted her position, laid her head upon Megara's lap and continued to stare at me though she was falling asleep. She looked so soft and gentle now with Megara pulling her long dark hair away from her head and letting it fall. Cinnamon's hand floated through the air and brushed gently against the head of a snake that she seemed to know was there without looking. It seemed strange to me that this was the same girl that just an hour earlier was spinning somersaults in the air in the sweaty hold of the ship. Now, she looked like a girl in a painting. She was so pretty. As Megara brushed Cinnamon's hair and spoke words to me that I wasn't really hearing, Cinnamon's eyes shut and she fell asleep. It was time to go.

I stood up and tried to shake the sleep from my eyes.

"Do you have to go?" said Megara.

"Ummm . . . yes. Yes, we have to . . . uhh, sail tonight. Would you please tell Cinnamon that we will see her in Saipan?"

"I will. Please do come. She likes you. She never has anyone her own age to spend time with. And I know her; she will wait for you every day."

"I'll come. I promise. Goodbye."

I took one last look at Megara's eyes. There was definitely something hypnotic about them. I pulled Hollie onto my back, went out and closed the door behind me. I was careful not to let any snakes out.

Chapter 17

MR. CHEE HAD told me to meditate. And I had promised to try. So, I turned the lights low, lit a candle and sat on a blanket by the observation window. Hollie and Seaweed sat beside me and watched.

First, I practised breathing the way he showed me, which was pretty much what I always did before I free dived, as it helped me dive deeper, which was what I was really looking forward to doing again as soon as my arm was well enough. It had been such a long time, and I hadn't been able to dive in the Arctic. I had learned to dive to a hundred feet, but found I could dive deeper in warmer water than cold, so was curious to see how deep I could dive in the Pacific. Anyway,

I was supposed to empty my mind and focus on the idea of living a life less dangerous.

I shut my eyes and tried to empty my mind. Suddenly, I remembered the polar bear trying to squeeze his nose into the portal. Whew! That was a close one. Then I remembered being stuck in the ice for three days. Funny, it had felt like much longer at the time, like forever. Now, it didn't seem such a big deal. Imagine what the crew of the Franklin expedition must have gone through.

Concentrate! I told myself. Empty your mind. I breathed more deeply. The image of the fishing trawler drifted into my head. I wondered if it had reached bottom yet. Probably. And the pressure would have crushed the hull together like a tin can. And the sailors? And the man who had shot me? Did they drown right away or had they survived for a while in that lifeboat? What a horrible thing to happen. Was that really karma, or was that just bad luck? And those waves; how big did they really get? Stop thinking! Empty your mind.

I breathed deeply, opened my eyes and peeked at the candle. The light reflected off Hollie's eyes. How frightening it must have been for him to have been chased by that snake. I imagined the snake sneaking into the sub, so quietly Hollie wouldn't even have heard it. Snakes are surely the scariest hunters. Would Hollie have smelled it? Probably he started barking but nobody heard him. Then Seaweed heard him and he flew down and started squawking, trying to warn me. Hollie and Seaweed were fiercely protective of each other, in spite of their fussiness. The snake would have gone for Hollie, and Hollie must have jumped out of the way. Then, he ran to the ladder, which he once had climbed, but couldn't get up fast enough to escape the snake so he ran into the engine compartment, and the snake followed . . . Stop thinking! Empty your mind!

I shut my eyes again and breathed more deeply. I wondered where we should go next. Saipan, of course, but there was another place I wanted to visit on the way: Bikini Atoll. It was the most contaminated place in the world. Dozens of atomic bombs had been exploded there in the 1940s and '50s. The first hydrogen bomb was exploded there too and it was so powerful it had vaporized three islands. They don't exist anymore. Wow. How does an island vaporize? Bikini Lagoon is still there though. It's a graveyard for warships now. Cool. Bikini Atoll is in the Marshall Islands, which is where Amelia Earhart probably went down. If her plane is under water, it's probably somewhere in the Marshall Islands. Hey! Maybe if I try really hard I can find it. I don't have to worry about ice here . . . Concentrate! Boy, I would really like to find Amelia Earhart's plane. Concentrate!! Nah . . . forget it. I can't. I jumped up, blew out the candle and hit the lights. I couldn't meditate. There were just too many things to do.

According to my map and compass readings, we were about twenty-four hundred miles due west of Hawaii, and the same distance from Japan, in the opposite direction. We were just two hundred miles west of Wake Island, a tiny island with an American Air Force and missile base. I figured it was probably not a good idea to sail any closer than we already were, even though chances were, with all their sophisticated detection systems, they already knew we were here and were watching us. So, I set a course, cranked up the engine, climbed the portal with Hollie and headed due south towards Bikini Atoll.

The horizon was turning blue. The sky in the Pacific was different from the sky in the Atlantic or Arctic. It had more colour than the Atlantic and was bigger than the Arctic. I didn't know if that were true but it sure felt like it. We saw a bird. It came out of nowhere in the night sky. We could just make out its silhouette against the blue. It was flying alone. How far it must have come. Where would it land? I thought of Amelia Earhart again. She had been flying these skies when she went down. It was at night. I read that her plane, a Lockheed Electra, twin-engine, would only be travelling at thirty-five miles an hour when it landed on a runway. At that speed she could easily have survived a landing in the water. Her plane probably wouldn't have broken apart. But it would have sunk. Probably it was still in one piece somewhere.

The bird looked so lonely I couldn't stop watching it. Hollie watched it too. Why would one bird fly so far all by itself?

When the sun came up I cut the engine and slowed to a drift. The water looked inviting. Sometimes the nicest thing was to dive from the top of the portal into the water. It was something you should never do in a lake or river or anywhere with dark water that you couldn't see through, because you might strike something. Out in the middle of the Pacific Ocean, where the floor was a couple of miles down, that was unlikely.

But my arm was too sore to dive or even jump, so I slipped off the hull a bit clumsily and had an easy swim a few times around the sub, using just my legs and one arm. The water was so warm—it was wonderful. I closed my eyes. Suddenly, my foot struck something and it scared the heck out of me. I immediately thought of sharks and scrambled up the side of the sub. I turned around and looked into the water but didn't see anything. That was weird.

I went inside and peeked at the sonar screen. There was nothing. Nothing on radar either. Was it a shark? I didn't see any fins. There would have been fins.

I had to know what it was so I turned on battery power and slowly motored around in circles. I didn't see anything from the portal. Then, I got an idea. I went inside and looked down through the observation window. Sure enough, there was some kind of dull grey shape there, just hanging in the water, not really floating and not sinking. I couldn't tell how big it was or what it was made of. It looked like plastic, but wouldn't plastic float on the surface?

I kneeled down at the window and stared at the grey blob. Should I move on or should I investigate? I looked at Hollie.

He was curious because I was curious. "Okay. I'll investigate."

I took a twenty-foot length of rope, tied it to the gaff and threw the gaff over the side. After a few tries I hooked on to something. I pulled up slowly by leaning back with the rope over my shoulder, then wrapping the rope around the portal so it wouldn't sink. But whatever it was didn't want to sink anyway. What on earth was it?

It broke the surface like a chunk of dead, rotted flesh. But I was right, it was plastic. It was about eight feet long, three feet wide and maybe four feet deep. It had no markings on it, nothing to identify it at all. It must have been in the ocean so long everything had faded. Now it was nothing but a grey blob. I unhooked it and let it go. But it didn't go anywhere. I went back inside, shut off the lights and went to bed. I made a feeble attempt at meditating in bed but fell asleep.

In the early twilight when I woke, we were surrounded by a sea of plastic.

It must have been garbage dumped out of a ship. There should have been a law against that—dumping at sea—but I didn't think there was, although I would sometimes see a sign posted in harbours prohibiting dumping in the water. Everywhere around us were plastic bottles, plastic bags, round plastic, straight plastic, crooked plastic, plastic rope, plastic netting and on and on. There were also broken pieces of industrial-looking plastic. Some of it was in large globs like the piece we found before going to bed, but most of it was in smaller chunks. Why would a ship dump plastic garbage into the sea? Oh! Maybe the ship had been caught in that typhoon and sank. Hmmm. Except that this garbage was really old and deformed. It looked like it had been in the water for many, many years.

We motored slowly through the garbage as the twilight turned darker. I didn't want to run into anything bigger. But none of the garbage seemed an obstacle to the sub. I couldn't believe how long the trail lasted. We were still seeing it when it grew dark. It was so depressing! It reminded me of what Nanuq, the old Inuit man, had said about the sea dying. I was glad he couldn't see this. Garbage made the ocean look like a dump, or like a dead swamp or an industrial lake. I was glad when the darkness hid it from us. In the morning, when the sun came up, the sea would be fresh and clean.

It wasn't! I couldn't believe it. The garbage continued forever in all directions. This was scary. What was going on?

I went inside and looked down through the observation window. The garbage was at least twenty to thirty feet deep. There were chunks here and there, but there was also a kind of sludge in the water, like melted ice, except it was plastic.

A little while later there was a really bad smell on the port side. It was so foul I had to cover my nose. Hollie smelled it and looked worried. I saw netting in the water. Then, I saw carcasses. There were turtles, dolphins, sharks and fish all rotting in the sun. It was a net just like the one I had broken, but nobody had rescued these creatures. Hugh wasn't here.

There were no transmitters on any of the turtles.

I couldn't get away from the smell. It was so bad I threw up over the side. Then we passed the area and the air was fresh again. But the garbage continued. It continued all day. In the late afternoon we came across another carcass tied up in part of a net. It was the headless torso and part of the legs of a man. I stopped the sub, backed up and stared at the body. If we were back in Canada I would have reported it. But who would I call here? Who would come all the way out here for part of a dead body? Nobody. Nobody would care. As I stared at the corpse I felt that something had changed inside of me. I didn't know what it was exactly and couldn't have put it in words, but I didn't feel there was much difference between the plastic garbage and the dead body. I wasn't sure that was the right way to feel about it but I couldn't help it. Everything here was dead. Everything was rotting. What was the difference?

Well, it was a body. It had been somebody. I should have felt sad for the person. It *was* sad. And yet, it looked like just another piece of garbage. The garbage really scared me. I was afraid that Nanuq was right; the sea was dying. The sea was certainly dying here. We were killing its creatures and we were dumping our garbage into it. We were killing it.

Chapter 18

ON THE SECOND day of garbage I was sick to my stomach with worry. I had sailed past dozens of carcasses of dolphins, turtles, sharks, even a small whale. Some had been caught in nets and drowned. Pieces of netting floated with them, wrapped around them. With some I couldn't tell what had killed them. They were all drifting with the garbage and rotting under the sun. There weren't any smaller fish eating them as there would have been in cleaner, healthier water. I was worried to death. And then, for the first time since we left the circus ship, I heard a beep on the radar. Thank heavens, I thought! I would go out of my mind all alone out here.

The vessel was ten miles away when it hopped onto the radar screen. I sailed straight towards it. I wanted to know what it was. I didn't care about submerging. I was too upset.

She was a small ship, about the size of a coastguard ship. I could tell from five miles away through binoculars. But I couldn't see any markings. It was twilight by the time we were close enough for her to spot us. She would have seen us on radar at the same time we had seen her. I didn't know what she was doing here but I knew it wasn't fishing. The only thing you could fish for here was garbage.

As it turned out, that's what she was doing. When I drew the binoculars across her bow I read, "Environmental Protection Ship – *Phoenix*."

I felt a burst of hope. She was here to clean up the garbage! Then I thought for a moment: how could she do that? The garbage stretched forever. She was just one small ship. Still, the fact that she was here filled me with hope. It meant that somebody knew about it; somebody cared. I pulled up under the shadow of her bow, cut the engine, climbed the portal and stood up. There were half a dozen people on deck leaning over, staring, smiling and waving. They had watched us come in.

"Ahoy! Submariner! Ahoy! Where are you from?"

"Canada."

"What brings you out here?"

"I'm exploring."

The sound of voices brought Seaweed up the portal. He took a quick peek and jumped into the air. Then Hollie wanted up. I climbed down and carried him up.

"Will you come aboard?"

"Yes. Thank you."

They dropped a rope ladder. I tied up to it, put Hollie in the tool bag and swung it over my shoulder. I couldn't wait to get on deck and ask them about the garbage. But climbing the ladder was difficult. I could only hold on with one arm.

There were seven people on deck: four men and three women. They told me their names and I told them mine but I couldn't remember any of theirs, except for one, Carl, who was older than the others and probably from Sweden. He was one of those sailors who spent so much time in the sun his face looked like an old leather boot. He was waiting at the top of the ladder to help me up. "You're just a lad! What happened to your arm?"

"I uhh . . . was shot."

I had to bite my lip, not because I had been shot but because I had been sailing through garbage for a day and a half and it felt like it was the end of the world. I hadn't realized how upset I really was.

"Ho! How did it happen?"

"I was freeing turtles and dolphins from a trawler net."

"Oh! Good for you! And they shot you?"

"Yes."

He looked angry enough to kill somebody himself. "Shrimp trawlers! They're the scum of the earth! Let me see it."

I raised my arm. He lifted the bandage and looked at the

wound. It was covered with a scab. I would carry a deep scar for the rest of my life. I didn't care.

"You realize they were trying to kill you, right?"

"Yes."

"They'll kill anything that gets in their way, anything between them and their pursuit of money."

"But why do they kill turtles and dolphins? If they're after shrimp, why don't they let everything else go?"

"They're supposed to! They're supposed to have holes in their nets that let the turtles, dolphins and sharks escape. But they don't work very well and they get impatient. The turtles get tangled in the nets. The dolphins and sharks too. Rather than look for a humane solution, they just slaughter them and discard them. It's madness. They're murderers! They don't care. But it's only short-term gain. In the long run they're killing the very food chain that's feeding them. We're in a fight to save the oceans, my friend. It's a fight between those who want to make a fast dollar and those who want to save the planet."

I looked around at their staring faces. These were the people who wanted to save the planet.

"But what about this garbage? Do you know where it has come from? Do you know why there is so much here?"

Carl nodded up and down and frowned. "This, my friend, is an island of plastic the size of Texas. Some say it's twice as big as that. We're not really sure. We call it an island but it's more like a carpet, as you can see. You can't stick your hand into the water without touching something. It's here because plastic floats. It breaks down into smaller and smaller pieces but it never biodegrades. So, it's always here. The island has been growing since the 1950s at least. Every day it pulls more plastic into it like a black hole, except that it doesn't disappear, it grows."

He picked up a jar of sea water. "See how murky it is? It looks like silt, right? Well, those are particles of plastic. The fish eat that and they die. Dolphins eat it, sharks eat it, turtles eat it, whales eat it, seabirds eat it. They all die."

He slammed the jar down with a bang.

"But . . . where does the plastic come from? And why is it *here*?"

Carl raised his hands in front of his face and spun them in circles in opposite directions. "We are in a vortex. The currents of the Pacific spin like wheels, this way and that, around and around, but here, they don't spin. This is the centre. Not the geographic centre, just the centre of the currents. The garbage gets swept here by the currents, becomes trapped and just stays. You can find pieces of plastic here that were thrown into the sea fifty years ago."

"Wow."

"Yet most of the world doesn't even know it's here."

"Can't we tell everyone?"

"We're trying. You'd be amazed how difficult it is to get people to hear something they don't want to hear. The average person contributes about two hundred pounds of plastic to the garbage of the world every year. That's a *lot* of plastic. Since it doesn't biodegrade, it has to end up some-where. A lot of it ends up here. But since people don't see it, they don't care about it."

"If it kills the oceans they will care."

"Yes, but by then it will be too late."

The *Phoenix* was part of an international environmental protection organization. Each of the crew was a researcher from a North American or European university. One of the women was from the University of British Columbia in Van-couver. She was studying the effects of ocean garbage on sea turtles. I told her about Hugh and asked her if she put transmitters on turtles. She said no, but other people did. Then she asked me about my sub. "Are you a . . . I mean, you're so young and everything, but . . . are you a vigilante environmentalist or something?"

"No. I'm an explorer."

"But you're fighting with fishing trawlers. And you just got shot. And you're way out in the middle of the Pacific Ocean all by yourself, except for a dog. Or did we see a sea-gull climb out of your submarine too?"

"Yes. That's Seaweed. He's my first mate. Hollie is my sec-ond mate."

I opened the tool bag and lifted Hollie out. His tail was wagging like a ribbon flapping in the wind. She patted him while he tried to give her a bath with his tongue. "What a cutie! Please, come inside and let me take a closer look at your arm."

I followed her inside the cabin, sat down at a table and let her unwrap the bandage and examine my arm. She took my temperature, felt my pulse and measured my blood pressure.

"Are you a doctor?"

"No, but I studied to be a paramedic before I studied oceanography. When did it happen?"

"About ten days ago."

"Can you use your hand?"

"A little bit. It's getting better slowly. I had acupuncture a few times on another ship."

"You had acupuncture out here? That's funny. One moment you get shot, the next you get acupuncture. That's the Pacific for you. I can give you some tablets for pain if it starts to hurt again. And I can give you an antiseptic cream to rub over it. That will help protect it from infection. You're doing a good job keeping it clean. How old are you?"

"Sixteen."

"Pretty young to be so far from home all by yourself. Where are your parents?"

"My father lives in Montreal. I was raised by my grandparents in Newfoundland. I left home at fourteen."

"Have you been at sea ever since then?"

"Pretty much. I visit with friends a lot."

"Where did you get the submarine?"

"I made it with somebody. I had a lot of help."

She paused while she watched the blood pressure gauge. "Your story is amazing. I have a nephew who's sixteen—I wish he could see what you are doing with your life. Someone like you could really make a difference in the world, Alfred, if you don't get killed first. It's dangerous out here."

"I know."

"Yes, I guess you do. Do you ever think of what you might do when you finish exploring?"

"No."

"Perhaps you should consider environmental protection. You obviously care a lot about animals and the environment. And we sure could use you on our side."

I nodded my head but didn't say anything. I wanted to think about it.

"I hope you will think about it. Where are you going next?"

"Bikini Atoll. Then Saipan."

"Boy! You're not exactly looking for the pleasure spots, are you?"

"I guess not."

I stayed just a few hours on the ship. When the crew started to get sleepy I thanked them for their help, climbed down the rope ladder and sailed away. They were going to bed but it was our morning. Besides, I had even more things to think about now.

By sunrise we had sailed free of the island of plastic. According to the crew of the *Phoenix*, we had passed through just one corner of it. I was so happy to see clean water again my heart lifted and my hopes did too. I couldn't stop thinking about what the woman from Vancouver had said: that I should consider a career in environmental protection. I loved the sea with all my heart. I planned to spend my whole life on it. I wanted to protect it and all the creatures that lived in it: the turtles, whales, polar bears, seabirds, dolphins, sharks. I wanted to stop the trawlers from killing everything in their way. I wanted to stop people from polluting the sea. Maybe Ziegfried could invent something to help clean it up. Perhaps he could design a ship that would suck up plastic, recycle it and filter the water until it was clean again. World War Two minesweepers searched for and gathered up explosive mines that had been dumped into the sea during the war. And they found most of them. Couldn't a ship do the same thing with plastic?

Maybe I could be both an explorer *and* an environmentalist. Why not? I would ask Ziegfried and Sheba their opinion, although I could guess what they would say. Both lived in houses full of animals and birds they had rescued. Both were dedicated to living in ways that didn't harm the environment. They would like it.

Chapter 19

AS WE SAILED SOUTH to Bikini Atoll the sun grew hotter every day. The hull heated up so much I had to carry a t-shirt up and lay it on the metal when I wanted to lean against the hatch. How hot could it get?

Bikini Atoll is the top of a seamount that broke the surface in several places, each one creating a tiny island. Bikini Island is the biggest of them, although it is still pretty small. The islands form an oval, with a lagoon in the middle twenty miles long and ten miles wide. We were in the Marshall Islands now, where Amelia Earhart probably crashed into the sea before she was picked up by Japanese sailors and taken to Saipan. That was one theory. Perhaps she actually drowned. Nobody knew for sure. Saipan is also in Micronesia but a thousand miles away, on the other side of the Marianas Trench, the deepest seafloor in the world. Nothing about the Pacific is small.

Earhart left New Guinea in her small twin-engine plane and planned to land and refuel on Howland Island, a tiny island halfway to Hawaii. But she couldn't find it. She sent a few broken radio transmissions from her plane saying she couldn't find the island in the dark so she was flying north. But she was running out of gas. She probably tried to make it to the Marshall Islands, which are in a straight line between New Guinea and Hawaii, but were occupied by Japan at the time. Since the Japanese were preparing for war against the Americans they probably thought she was a spy.

Islands like Bikini are not easy to spot at sea because they are so small and flat. They don't have hills or mountains, and, like Sable Island, are often surrounded by rocky reefs that trick even the most experienced sailors. How many thousands of sailors had been shipwrecked on gentle looking islands? The lucky ones would have made it to shore, if they were able to swim, then spent the rest of their lives as castaways. That's what some people believe happened to Earhart: that she crashed close enough to an island to make it onto the beach, then lived as a castaway until she died. But maybe she crashed into the jungle of an island. No one will ever know—at least not until someone finds her plane.

Bikini Lagoon was one place I just had to see, even

though it was supposed to be the most contaminated place on earth, and you couldn't eat anything that grew there, not even the fish. And you'd get radiation poisoning if you hung around too long. I was dying to see it. In 1946, the Americans sailed seventy-six warships there and moored them in the lagoon. Then they detonated a couple of atomic bombs. They wanted to see if a navy could survive a nuclear attack.

Ten of the ships sank right away. Fifty-three were so hot with radiation they had to be towed to deeper water and sunk. One of them, the USS *Arkansas*, a huge battleship, was lifted vertically into the air during the explosion. Wow. The Americans set off over twenty atomic bombs on Bikini Atoll in twelve years. Then, they detonated a hydrogen bomb. That vaporized three islands. They don't exist anymore.

Twenty-three giant warships are still lying on the bottom of Bikini Lagoon, untouched since the bombs exploded. The biggest one, the USS *Saratoga*, was an aircraft carrier eight hundred and fifty feet long, just a few feet short of the *Titanic*. She was bigger than Sheba's island. And yet she could cut thirty-three knots through the water. That was unbelievable. She would have looked like an island racing across the sea. Now, she was lying on her keel, her bridge just forty feet beneath the surface.

I had to see that.

Another thing Bikini Lagoon was famous for, according to my guidebook, was its sea life. Since all the Bikinians had been taken away and relocated somewhere else, and no one fished there because no one could eat the fish, the lagoon was so full of sea life it was like nowhere else on earth. That was ironic.

All I wanted to do was sneak into the lagoon, have a look around and sneak out. It shouldn't be too difficult to do. The lagoon was ringed with sandbars like a lasso but my map showed that there was open water on the south side between the tiny islands. The atoll was uninhabited, except for occasional tourists and divers. I planned to sail in at night, have a look around when the sun came up, then sail out.

When the seafloor began to rise into a seamount I felt excited, even though it was a couple of hours before we saw anything. Hollie was excited too. He could smell land.

Eventually I saw a few scattered trees that looked as though they were sticking out of water from the distance. Probably they were coconut trees. They grew in the sand. You wouldn't know they were contaminated to see them. Now I could guess how the three islands had been vaporized. They were made of sand. The explosion just blew all that sand up into the sky, it drifted away in clouds, then rained down on the sea over hundreds or thousands of miles, like ashes from a volcano. That's what I imagined, anyway.

It was hours before dark but Hollie wanted out so badly that I dropped anchor off the sandbar, inflated the dinghy and rowed to shore. I was surprised there weren't any old shipwrecks here, since the sandbar was invisible from the sea. Without sonar there was no way to know it was even here. On the other hand, how many sailing ships would have come across the Pacific this way? And if there had been any old wrecks they probably would have been vaporized too. In any case, there was nothing here but sand, and no sounds but the lapping of waves on the beach. Even the sound of our feet in the sand was swallowed up in the vastness and I couldn't hear it. Hollie ran down the beach and he was the only thing that didn't look like sand. In the other direction there was a coconut tree. I walked that way.

It was hot! The sand was so hot I had to walk where it was wet. Seaweed landed on top of the coconut tree. Maybe the sand was too hot for him too. What a weird place. It was so quiet and empty. I stopped and turned around. This was the spot where over twenty nuclear bombs had been detonated. It was so peaceful now it was hard to imagine. Hollie started running towards me. He was still far away and he made no sound. This was surely one of the quietest places on earth.

After we returned to the sub, we sailed to the south side of the lagoon and waited until dark. Once twilight had appeared, darkness came quickly. We stood in the portal and watched the sun sink into the sea. Pacific sunsets were more spectacular than any other ones I had ever seen. They turned from yellow to purple, with shades of orange, red and every other colour in between, but mostly yellow and purple. And the colours spread out in shapes like wings and sails and long rolling scarves. I wondered if there was so much colour because of the heat.

When the last traces of colour disappeared I shut the hatch, submerged to periscope depth and entered the lagoon. I didn't enter on the surface because I didn't want any vessels that might be there to know by radar that we had come in.

The floor of the lagoon was a hundred and eighty feet deep and was a smooth and sandy surface. I picked up what I thought was a rocky promontory on sonar but as we motored closer I realized it was one of the ships. I couldn't believe how big it was. It was almost a thousand feet long, which meant it must have been the *Saratoga*. I felt butterflies in my stomach.

I wanted to touch the deck of the ship, which was ninety feet down. Although I could dive a hundred feet, I only had one good arm. And there were lots of sharks around. And it was the most contaminated place in the world, or used to be, even though it didn't look it. I also didn't want to get spotted and chased out of the lagoon by a bunch of excited tourists in fancy speedboats.

We hovered above the *Saratoga* and I hit the floodlights. I couldn't see much, even though she was right outside the window. She was too big and we were too close. I decided to motor around and locate some of the other ships. There was an airplane next to the *Saratoga*, which must have blown from her deck or hangar when the bomb went off.

I scouted around for a few hours, found two submarines and a bunch of huge ships which on sonar looked like monsters sleeping in the lagoon. There were so many of them. It was really spooky. I couldn't wait for the sun to come up.

When it did, I was sitting on the hull with the hatch wide open. We were right above the *Saratoga* again. There was no current in the lagoon so I felt no need to drop anchor. Besides, I didn't want to get it tangled up in an aircraft carrier.

Morning is when sharks like to feed, but sharks, as a rule, don't make a habit of eating people, especially small to medium sized sharks. I wasn't expecting to see any great white sharks here, though I'd be watching closely. Hollie was sitting at the bottom of the ladder looking up. He wanted another run in the sand, and he would get one soon. Seaweed was sitting on the hull. He looked like he was thinking, "What are we doing here?"

"I just want to make a few dives, you guys. Then we'll go."

I went inside, took off my t-shirt, sneakers and bandage. Ziegfried had said that, though the water here was contaminated, it wouldn't hurt to dive a few times. I figured the salt water would be good for my wound. I went back out. The sun was coming up over the horizon. It streaked across the water. The water was so blue! I climbed down onto the hull and got a fright. The *Saratoga* lay beneath us as clear as could be and she was so enormous I couldn't believe it. It looked as though I could just reach down and touch her. But there was movement in the water all around her. I slipped into the water and saw thousands of fish disappear in a flash, then return just as quickly. Schools of them turned together with lightning speed. I saw sharks further below over the edge of the deck. Further below that I saw the airplane sitting on the lagoon floor, one hundred and eighty feet down!

The water was thirty degrees Celsius, or eighty-five degrees Fahrenheit. It was like a bathtub. I remembered falling in the Arctic Ocean and turning numb in less than a minute. Arctic water might be cleaner, but it sure would kill you a lot faster.

The deck was ninety feet down but the bridge was only forty, off to one side. I decided to dive to the bridge first. I took some deep breaths, calmed myself and went under.

My arm was still very sore, and I had to use my left hand more and kick harder with my feet. I swam about twenty feet in an angle towards the bridge, then up again. Now it was directly below me. I poked my head out of the water. There were no tourist boats around yet. I took a deep breath and went under.

It felt very strange touching the metal skin of such an enormous ship. The guidebook said that the *Saratoga* had been torpedoed several times yet survived. When the war ended she carried home more troops than any other ship: hundreds of thousands of soldiers. Then, she was ordered to take part in the atomic tests here. But she didn't survive that. She might have if they had been able to climb inside and bail her and fix the leaks. But they couldn't touch her; she was too hot with radiation. All they could do was sit back and watch as she sank. And it took eight hours before she slipped beneath the waves and settled on the bottom. She has been lying here ever since. Touching her gave me a creepy feeling, as if I were touching a mechanical giant from another planet.

Maybe any moment her lights would come on and she would start to rise. Now that was a scary thought.

It took forty-five minutes and six dives to reach her deck. It was a lot harder with only one good arm. When my feet touched the deck I looked up. Ninety feet above, on the surface, the sub looked so small. Schools of fish swam above me in walls of bright colour. When the sun streaked through the water they looked like they were on fire. Sharks glided among them like miniature black submarines, but calmly. This was a place with lots of food. The sharks were well fed.

Back on the sub I sat on the hull and stared across the lagoon. Two thoughts ran through my mind. I loved machines. I was in awe of big mechanical giants like the *Saratoga*. They fascinated me. I thought they were beautiful in an odd way. This lagoon was full of them. It was like a museum of monstrous mechanical inventions. It was probably the oddest museum you could ever visit. That was one thought.

The other thought was that all of these machines were designed to kill. They weren't *only* designed to kill, but that was a big part of what they could do. Why was I so excited about things that were designed to kill? That didn't feel right. What made them any different from the bad shrimp trawlers or the pollution that was killing the sea? All of these things were bad. And yet, I liked the machines. And that confused me.

I remembered Ziegfried once telling me that there was a world of difference between weapons in the hands of people like Hitler, and weapons in the hands of people fighting against him. "If we hadn't stopped Hitler, Al," he had said, "we'd all be living in a tyranny. All the Jews of the world would be dead, so would millions of other people Hitler didn't like. And in the Pacific, if we hadn't stopped the Japanese Emperor, we'd all be servants of an autocracy. Freedom's a precious thing, Al. Now, Japan and Germany are two of the richest countries in the world, and they're free, like us. But we had to fight them back then, Al, when they were ruled by dictators. And we had to use weapons. We had no choice."

I wished I had pointed out that if there were no weapons in the first place, Hitler and the Emperor would never have become so powerful. But it only occurred to me just now. On the other hand, if we didn't have mechanical machines, I wouldn't have my sub. As I rested my head on my knees and stared across the lagoon at the sun sparkling on the tiny waves, I sighed. I missed Ziegfried.

Chapter 20

I WOKE FROM THE deepest sleep. For a moment I didn't know where we were. Were we in the Arctic? I sure hoped not. No, we couldn't be. I remembered the *Saratoga*. How long had we slept? I raised my head. Seaweed was sitting on his spot like a statue. Where was Hollie? I had the vague feeling I had lost him. Had I lost him? I looked under my cot. No, he was there, chewing his rope. Thank heavens. I lay back down. Then I remembered. We were outside of Bikini Lagoon. We walked on the beach for hours. I had got sunburnt. Hollie had too, or maybe it was sunstroke. Anyway, we had crawled into the sub, submerged a hundred feet off the beach, dropped into bed and fell asleep. That was fourteen hours ago. It was time to get up. It was time to sail to Saipan.

I felt like an old man getting up and putting on the kettle. Seaweed shook out his feathers. That was his way of stretching. I stretched too. Then Hollie did, though he didn't need to. He was already awake and ready to go. I looked up at my chin-up bar. Was my arm strong enough yet? I climbed up and hung from the bar. That felt good. I did three chin-ups before my arm felt too sore to continue. That wasn't too bad. It was getting better.

After breakfast I had my first small successful meditation, though it was probably only because I was still too sleepy to think about anything yet. Then we surfaced to greet the brilliant sunshine.

But it wasn't there.

I felt the toss of waves even before I opened the hatch. When I opened it the wind howled above me and rain lashed against my face. Seaweed started up the ladder then went back down. I turned to look at the beach and saw the coconut trees bending in the wind. I couldn't believe this was the same place where we had walked on the beach hours before without the merest breath of wind. Was this the start of a typhoon? If it were, I wanted to sail out of it. I didn't feel like fighting with a typhoon. It would last for days. Nor did I want to keep the crew cooped up the way we were in the Arctic. Since the wind was coming from the east, I turned south and cranked up the engine. We would ride the surface as long as we could, then go under.

We sailed twenty hours straight. Half that time we spent on the surface and half beneath. I rode the bike for a few hours, Hollie ran on the treadmill and Seaweed did a little too. I groomed Hollie's fur, attempted to groom Seaweed's feathers, meditated a little, spent some time reading, tried to reach Ziegfried and sent a message to Angel and hoped she received it. After twenty hours I went back to sleep.

This time I set the alarm for four hours. I wanted to stay ahead of the storm, or rather, south of it, because the sky was darkest to the north. The winds were blowing steadily from the east. I believed we were escaping the worst of it by continuing south. But who knew what a typhoon would do?

The second day was rough, though not as rough as it might have been. There was one remarkable difference between a storm here and a storm anywhere else: here it was warm, both the water and wind. It made everything feel a lot less dangerous. But that was deceiving. It didn't feel threatening to fall overboard because you could float in the water all day if you had to, especially if you had something to hold on to. At least you wouldn't die of exposure right away. But you would still die, eventually, in the vastness.

Since we were sailing due south I figured we were cutting through the Ralik Chain, a string of seamounts and atolls on the western border of the Marshall Islands. But with the tossing and pitching of the storm, and poor visibility, I wasn't actually certain where we were. All I knew for sure was that we were sailing south.

We came close to an island once. Sonar told me to steer

west of it or we'd smash into the reef. I wondered: were we on the north side of Namorik Atoll, or Pingelap? Was it somewhere else? I really didn't know. I was confused because the wind had changed, but it was hours before I realized it had happened. Now it was blowing from the north. The storm was following us. Rats. We couldn't keep running from it; it would just chase us all around the Pacific. I decided to head northwest, directly towards Saipan. I didn't want to miss the circus. But first, I needed to sleep.

We followed the rising seafloor upwards along a seamount towards a small atoll shaped like a horseshoe, though I didn't know which one it was. If we could sail into the lagoon, not only would we have shelter from the storm, we might get out for a walk on the beach.

The atoll was very small, just a couple of miles wide. I didn't recognize it from my charts. It must have been outside of the Marshall Islands. On the west side I found a shallow channel that we could only enter in high tide. So, we waited. Once we entered the lagoon I scouted around before settling. If there were people here we'd sail out before the tide turned. But there weren't. It was uninhabited. I was tempted to call it *Ziegfried Lagoon*.

I tossed the anchor in fifteen feet on the west side of the lagoon, a hundred feet from the beach. I inflated the dinghy, rowed to shore with Hollie, climbed out and tied the dinghy to a tree. Seaweed stayed inside the sub. It was storming pretty hard but there was a line of coconut trees on the beach and they led to a small jungle on a small rise on the north side.

Hollie was not the least bit put off by the storm, even though it blew his fur backwards and made it difficult for him to trot in a straight line—not that he was in the habit of trotting in a straight line. He stayed close to me and I stayed close to the trees. I was amazed at how much they bent in the wind, as if they were made of rubber.

We went up the rise, which was maybe seventy-five feet at its highest point. A tsunami would roll over this island as if it weren't even here. But there was a tiny area of jungle. It was only a quarter of a mile long and a few hundred feet wide, but it was a jungle. I had never actually seen a real one before.

The trees were close together and there were bushes and plants with big fat leaves everywhere. I didn't know if there were any snakes here, or spiders or dangerous animals. Probably not. We did see a large crab, and it was very aggressive. When Hollie sniffed at it, it lunged at him and he jumped back. That's when I picked him up. The plants were too thick and tall for him to jump over anyway, and I didn't want to lose sight of him. But even I had trouble getting through the bushes.

The jungle was growing out of rocky ground, very different from the sandy beaches that surrounded most of these atolls. Probably the rock was the remains of an old volcano. For such a tiny jungle, it was surprisingly difficult to get through. At one point I thought I had discovered a cave, but it was just an overhanging rock. It made a good shelter from the storm. Everything was moving in the wind. I had to tell myself to ignore the leaves and bushes because it looked so much like there were creatures running through them. And then, I made a discovery.

First, my foot struck what I thought was a heavy rock but turned out to be a chunk of metal. It was badly rusted but I could tell it was part of a machine, possibly an engine. Then, I found a cable. It had been here for a very long time. Next, I found part of a sheet of metal. And then, against the rock above thick bushes, I saw a propeller. My heart raced with excitement. It was an airplane.

It was a twin-engine plane. Amelia Earhart flew a twin-engine plane. I was so excited my heart was thumping in my chest. But the plane was difficult to reach, especially with Hollie in my arms and the storm blowing everything around. I decided to return to the sub, leave Hollie there and come back with the camera.

It grew darker as we returned to the sub. I hoped it wouldn't rain before I could take some photos. Hollie met up with another crab on the way back. This time he was determined to stare it down, but the crab got too close and grabbed hold of his fur with its pincers. The next thing I saw was the crab flying through the air. It was the most ferocious thing I had ever seen Hollie do, next to fighting off the snake. Seaweed would have ripped the crab apart.

Hollie was content to join Seaweed in the sub, especially as he brought a new stick in with him. I grabbed the camera and a plastic rain poncho that fit in my pocket, climbed out and shut the hatch behind me. I paddled over to the beach, tied up the dinghy and took off towards the jungle. It struck me: some years ago—day or night—the pilot of that plane had crashed here. He, or she, must have run out of gas. Why else would they have tried to land in a place with nowhere to land? Perhaps they had tried to land in the lagoon. It would be hard to see at night, impossible in fact, unless it was a clear night and there were stars and the moon. Then the atoll would look like a black horseshoe on a dark sea. Was I the first one to find the plane? Maybe. I was excited.

The little jungle swallowed me up. I learned that you can't hurry through a jungle; it is too thick. You have to climb over, around and under things. Hopefully there were no dangerous snakes. I couldn't see them if there were. There was nothing for them to eat here anyway, except crabs. I wondered what the crabs ate.

When I reached the rock face where the plane was, I started taking pictures right away. With the zoom lens I could see the frame of the cockpit. I had to get over there.

But it wasn't easy, especially with my sore arm. What a nuisance! I climbed up the rock, holding on to leaves and plant stems, but couldn't see where my feet were landing, as the plants were too thick. It was slippery too. If I fell, I probably would have landed in bushes, but many of them had sharp thorns. I wondered if there were dangerous ants here, as in the movies. I hadn't seen a single ant yet.

The plane was very beaten up. It must have hit the rock pretty hard. Perhaps it had exploded on impact. Plants grew tightly around it and right through the middle of it. I climbed on top. It was broken in two. I didn't see any markings anywhere as everything was so badly rusted. I couldn't even tell if it was a military or civilian plane. There probably wasn't a big difference back in the 1930s. I climbed forward towards the cockpit and saw that the glass was missing from the windows. I looked for remains of the pilot but there was nothing. The jungle was slowly eating the plane; perhaps something else had eaten the pilot. Then, I saw a boot. It was squashed into one corner. I pulled off a metal strip sticking up and stuck it into the corner and pulled the boot out. It was a small leather boot, all crumpled up. The pilot hadn't been very big. I opened up the boot and turned it upside down. Out fell dirt and a small pile of bones. They were the bones of a foot. I looked for the other boot but it wasn't there.

I took more photos from inside the plane and out. While I was aiming the camera, a heavy drop of rain splashed on my face. Shoot! It was time to go. I focused on the pilot's seat one last time and noticed something underneath it. I climbed in again, stuck my hand under the seat and pulled out a small leather bag with a strap. Black marks on the front of the bag looked like Japanese letters. I opened it and found badly faded maps and papers. The writing was in Japanese. It probably wasn't Amelia Earhart's plane. Too bad. Oh well, it was still a pretty cool discovery. It started to rain. I wrapped the camera and bag in the plastic poncho and climbed out of the plane. I left the boot behind.

Chapter 21

THE SEA WAS BUILDING swells slowly but steadily, as if it were taking its good old time preparing a typhoon. Rain fell on and off and the wind howled constantly. After a few days, riding the waves became exhausting and the vibration from storm choppiness was starting to wear on my nerves. So, we slipped beneath the waves and continued sailing in a northwest direction. Sailing submerged was slower, but so much more comfortable. We were not in any hurry anyway. I didn't want to miss the circus, but Pierre the strongman said they wouldn't set up until after the typhoon and clean-up were over. I wondered how you cleaned up after a typhoon.

We motored along at a hundred feet, coming up every four hours or so to charge the batteries and check the storm. The seafloor dropped below us to deeper than two miles, then, almost as soon as it bottomed out, it started up again. I watched it rise steadily on sonar. Although the horizon showed nothing in our path, we knew an island was coming, or at least a seamount.

We were at sea so long I was once again losing the feeling of sleeping in the night or day. It didn't really matter. It was too much to fuss over whether it was light or dark when I laid my head down. The sun set around seven in the evening and rose around seven in the morning every day here; that much I knew. I figured that was because we were so close to the equator.

The seamount continued to rise until radar told me it had broken the surface ten miles in front of us. There was an atoll ahead. This time it was much bigger. Likely there would be people. Perhaps we could settle on the bottom offshore, or perhaps we could find an isolated lagoon and take shelter.

Not a chance. The seamount rose into a jagged and dangerous reef all around the atoll, and the atoll was too big to bother circling for a safe entrance to its lagoon. Oh, well, I thought, we'll just settle outside the reef and sleep.

So we did. But while I slept, I heard sounds, soft scraping sounds, as if the sub were gently brushing against coral and debris on the bottom. But we were sitting at a hundred feet.

There couldn't be an undertow at a hundred feet, could there?

I drifted in and out of sleep and heard the scraping sounds as if they were far away. And then, there was a louder bang, and a clang, and a rumbling, like the sound of something sliding down a hill. I jumped to my feet, staggered over to the observation window and hit the floodlights. The water was murky with debris from the storm but it was clear enough to see movement outside. Where was this current coming from? And what were we banging into?

I climbed onto the bike and pedalled a little to change our position. Then I went back to the observation window. Looking down, I was staring at an airplane. I must be dreaming, I thought. But no, I wasn't. The plane looked similar to the one I had seen in the little jungle—a twin engine, but maybe a little bigger. It was hard to tell. Things look distorted underwater. The nose of the plane was missing. It looked jagged just like the rock around it. One of the engines was still attached and the other was nearby. The rest of the plane looked more or less intact.

I stood up, rubbed the sleep out of my eyes and tried to figure out what to do. Hollie stood up too and stared at me. We were a hundred feet down. There was a storm above and a dangerous reef in front of us. There was a flow of water coming from somewhere but I couldn't figure out where. I had just discovered another plane. Was this one Amelia Earhart's?

I put the kettle on, fed the crew, engaged the batteries and started exploring the area. We turned around and moved very slowly. Soon I discovered where the flow was coming from. There were holes in the reef. The water was channelling through them and creating a deep undertow.

I discovered something else. The reef was littered with machines and metal from the war. There must have been a battle here. I saw pieces of broken landing craft, the kind that carried soldiers onto the beach. I saw barrels, rods, cables and ripped sheets of metal that looked as though they had been torn apart by an angry giant.

And the plane? It was probably not Earhart's. It was probably another Japanese fighter. I had read that Japanese pilots often left their bases or aircraft carriers without enough fuel to return. After they had shot all their ammunition at the enemy they would crash their plane into an enemy ship or island. But some probably ran out of gas before they could do that. How many such planes were lying on the seafloor or in island jungles? Probably thousands of them.

World War Two started in 1939 and ended in 1945. But the Japanese and Americans only started fighting each other in 1941, after the Japanese attacked Pearl Harbor in Hawaii. They took the Americans by surprise. This was the beginning of four years of vicious fighting in the Pacific, which ended only when the Americans dropped the atomic bomb on Hiroshima and Nagasaki. But before the Americans could take the bomb all the way to Japan, they needed to find an island suitable enough for building an airfield from which their big bombers could take off. The island had to be close enough to Japan that the bombers could fly over, drop their bombs and fly back. That island turned out to be Tinian, right beside Saipan, an island in Japanese possession. To turn Tinian into an airfield—the biggest one in the world in 1945—the Americans first had to take Saipan. And so they did. But it took a whole month of really bloody fighting.

For two more days we battled the storm. I was so tired of it now. Then, suddenly, the wind just died. That was strange. It disappeared too quickly. It left an eerie stillness in its wake that I didn't trust. The sea still flowed in large swells but the swells lost their crests and we could ride them comfortably. I cranked up the engine and made a beeline for Saipan. The typhoon was still on its way; I could feel it. Even though the air was motionless, it was full of energy, sort of like the stillness before lightning strikes. How different this was from back home. At home, you might know a few days before a bad storm would hit or you might not know at all. In the Pacific, typhoons seemed to take weeks to form. They built in stages, then they moved around looking for somewhere to strike.

Chapter 22

WE WERE SITTING IN the water off Saipan, on the northeast side of the island. The wind and sea were throwing everything they had at it. The island looked like the dark green top of a giant's head sticking out of a steamy bath. Saipan had a small mountain in its centre that rose fifteen hundred feet. The typhoon might hit hard but the island wasn't going anywhere.

Finding a place to hide the sub might be a lot more difficult than I had thought. In the first place, I hadn't expected to come in the middle of a typhoon. We would need a very sheltered cove. But Saipan was highly populated for a Pacific island. There were about ninety thousand people here, according to my guidebook.

I couldn't search on the surface. The waves were too high, the wind too strong and the sky too dark. There was a lagoon on the east side but that was where all the people were. The north side was the least populated. It was also the hilliest. I would have to search here.

The undertows around the island were powerful and dangerous. I had never seen undertows like this before, not even in a storm. Something about the shape of the rock underwater was creating currents like in a washing machine. Maybe there were underwater tunnels. I felt an undertow pull us back and forth and had to be very careful not to smash into the reef. I sat at the sonar screen and studied the seafloor. After a while, I discovered something very cool. There were caves seventy-five feet down. I hovered above them, rushed to the observation window and looked down. There was a faint light coming through one of them. I stared at it and tried to figure out why. I could only guess that it was a cave on both sides. The water tunnel must have led to an open cave in the hillside where daylight was coming through. The tunnel looked big enough for the sub to squeeze through if we were careful. I decided to try it.

It was a tight squeeze. The tunnel led to a water-filled cave, like a giant well. There was plenty of light coming through the observation window. It must have been open above us. I rose very slowly. What if there were people sitting around the water at picnic tables? I didn't think it would be like that, especially with a typhoon developing, but it could have been.

We came up as slowly as possible. I raised the periscope, stopped and looked around. It was a cave all right, but one wall was completely open. I saw a small group of people huddled together and smoking in one corner. They didn't see us. I pulled the periscope down and we went back down just as slowly. We had to let air out of the tanks to submerge, and that made bubbles, so I did it as gently as possible not to draw attention. We couldn't hide in this cave, above or below, the water was too clear.

It was a tight squeeze getting out. Without sonar we would never have gotten in or out of that tunnel. As soon as we were out I found a second one. But there was no light coming from it. Should we check it out? I looked at the crew. Sometimes I wished they could talk. I decided to explore it.

It was longer and had a turn, which I didn't like. We scraped the sides coming through. It opened into an underwater cavern smaller than the other one. There was just enough room to turn the sub around. That was good; it would have been really hard to back up. I turned the sub as slowly as I could. I didn't want to hit the rock and cause a cave-in. I just hoped this cavern rose into a cave above water. If there was a cave above, there might be a way out of it.

We rose a little at a time. If we were going to hit a ceiling, I didn't want to hit it hard. Up, up, up we came. I raised the periscope gently. It broke the surface without striking anything but it was pitch-black. We were definitely in a cave. I surfaced completely and searched with the periscope again.

I turned it around three hundred and sixty degrees. It was like being in outer space, except without stars.

I was nervous to open the hatch. What if the air in the cave was stale? What if it was filled with poisonous gas? What if there were thousands of screaming bats, or poisonous spiders? I grabbed my guidebook and flipped through it. No, there were no dangerous spiders or snakes in Saipan. There was only the sea snake, an extremely venomous snake, but it was only in the water and it didn't like to bite. It preferred to swim inside dead bodies. That was nice.

I decided to open the hatch just a crack, shut it quickly, and hold my breath. I grabbed the flashlight, unsealed the hatch and readied myself. I pushed it up a tiny bit and shut it. Nothing happened. I heard nothing and smelled nothing. I opened it again a little further and pointed the flashlight out. It bounced off smooth stone walls. I took a breath. It was a little stale but okay so I opened the hatch and stuck my head out. I heard water drip. I swung the flashlight around in a circle. My mouth dropped. There were skeletons in here.

I didn't know if it was safe to flick on the floodlights. They were so bright. I didn't want to let anyone know we were here. But this cave must have been deep inside the ground. In fact, it must have been inside a hill. The presence of skeletons meant that nobody had been in here for a very long time. It was like a tomb. I decided to flick on the floodlights.

When the light burst into the room I saw five skeletons. They were in uniform. They weren't completely skeletons because they still had some skin on their bones—I could see it on their faces and hands—but it was dry and brown, sort of like the skin on mummies. They must have been Japanese soldiers. They weren't very big. They were spooky, but not incredibly spooky. I was more fascinated. I wondered what had happened to them. Had they come into the cave and couldn't get out? When I looked closer I saw that they all had white hair. Had they been here so long they had grown old? Or did their hair turn white because they had been frightened to death?

There were weapons here too. I saw rifles, pistols, boxes, cans and bottles. The skeletons were sitting around a card table. They must have gotten all of these things in here some-how, which meant that there must be a way out. I didn't think they could have come in the way we had come. But maybe they had. I could swim it, if I had to, if it were a matter of life and death. It was seventy-five feet down, fifty feet or so through a twisting tunnel and seventy-five feet back to the surface. And it was dark. Still, it was possible. Perhaps they had wrapped everything in plastic and swum through the underwater tunnels like a relay swimming team, passing their stuff from one person to another. Or maybe they pulled it through with ropes.

On one side of the cave was a ledge, like the boardwalk in-side a boathouse. That's where the skeletons were, with their boxes and things. The ceiling was about fifteen feet high. There was a rock at the back of the cave that looked as though it was blocking the entrance to a tunnel, but I couldn't tell. I'd have to go over there. To do that, I'd have to step past the skeletons.

I inflated the dinghy and shut off one of the floodlights. We didn't need that much light and I wanted to save power. Seaweed sat on the hull and watched as Hollie and I climbed into the dinghy and paddled ten feet to the ledge. The ledge was only five or six feet wide. Hollie jumped out. Then he stopped and stared at the skeletons. They were sitting at a card game, but beneath their uniforms they were just bone, hair and a little bit of skin. It was really weird. Their bones must have been balancing like wooden sticks that would collapse with the slightest touch or breeze, but there was absolutely no wind in the cave. I took a closer look at their faces. The leathery skin on their bones was as thin as a plastic bag pulled tight. I would have thought that skeletons all looked the same but they didn't. The holes of their eyes and noses were different sizes. Their cheekbones and foreheads were different. One looked braver than the others and one looked kind of funny. I wished Ziegfried was here. He would figure out what had happened to them and explain it to me.

They must have all died at the same time; otherwise, the ones who were living would have buried the ones who were dead. Skeletons are a lot scarier in movies than in real life. In real life they look more interesting than scary. It's probably because in the movies they make skeletons look as if they're alive, and that's frightening. In real life they're just dead. When something's dead, it's just dead, and it's not that scary if you look at it closely.

"It's okay, Hollie. But don't touch them."

He sniffed at the pant legs of two of them, sneezed, and we moved past. I wondered what they had died of. There were little tin cans on the table that looked burnt. Maybe they had been candles. Or had they, maybe, contained poison? Had the soldiers killed themselves? Had this been a planned suicide? From what I had read, it was more honourable for the Japanese to commit suicide than it was to surrender or get caught. I saw melted wax on the floor. There were kerosene lanterns too. I picked one up and shook it. Empty. I supposed they had run out, though it could have evaporated. What a dark and gloomy place this would have been to die. I sure was glad there were no signs of cannibalism.

Behind the rock was a passageway. You couldn't stand up in it unless you were really short. I shone the flashlight inside. The passage went straight a little bit then turned up. Hmmm. I looked at Hollie. He was sniffing it. He was curious. I looked behind us and saw Seaweed floating in the water. He looked content. I supposed we could investigate a little. I told myself: don't go farther than you know the way back. Don't get carried away with exploring and get lost.

Where the passageway went up there were edges of rock to hold on to, but I couldn't carry Hollie at the same time, so I went back to the sub and grabbed the tool bag. I took another flashlight too, just in case, and put it in a pocket in the side of the bag. Stepping past the skeletons each time was a little tricky. I tried very hard not to touch them but the tool bag slipped on my back, I lost my balance and gently bumped one. His skull rolled off his body and hit the rock with a sound like a hollow block of wood. "Sorry!" I said. I wondered if maybe I should put the skeletons into the water. That would be a kind of burial at sea. That's what I would have wanted. I would think about it first.

Where the passageway turned up I could use my hands and feet and go as slowly as I liked, which made it easier and I didn't have to use my sore arm as much. Holding the flashlight was tricky though. Once we made the first turn it became just as black behind us as in front of us. It was hot too. My hands started to sweat and that made them slippery.

The passage went up about ten feet and levelled out again. Now I had to crawl. It was only a couple of feet high. I didn't like that. But I was so curious I couldn't stop. I shone the light all around to make certain this was the only tunnel back to the cavern we came from. If we ever came to a section with two directions I would go back and do it all over again and make a map. I was *not* going to get lost.

It was stuffy because it was so hot. The slightest bit of work made you sweat. Hollie was panting in the bag. We crawled along for about twenty feet and went up again. It wasn't too hard because I moved slowly. You wouldn't want to come through here in a hurry. This time we went up farther, maybe twenty-five feet or so, and we had to climb around a rock in the centre. It was a tight squeeze. I felt shivers go up my spine. I would rather be under water than rock. I was more comfortable in water.

The passageway straightened once again and widened, which was a relief. It went about twenty feet then opened up into a cavern. Now I could stand up. I pointed the flashlight around the room. This was a cache. There were rifles, pistols, boxes, bottles, rolls of wire and leather bags. Happily, there were no skeletons. I took a good look around, although it was hard because the darkness ate up the light of the flashlight. You could only see where the light was pointing; the rest of the room was black. I sat down and rested. Climbing through caves was hard work, especially because it was so hot and stuffy. I decided to go back to the sub, get something to drink, clean up a bit, start a map and come back. I wanted to do everything in a calm, orderly way. It would keep me from getting too nervous.

I never got used to seeing the skeletons. Every time we entered the cavern they startled me. They didn't frighten me, they just startled me. I kept expecting to get used to them but never did. Seeing them made me feel that life was short. One minute you were alive, the next you weren't. That made me think of Mr. Chee. He said try to live a life less dangerous. How? Seeing the skeletons made me feel that living was dangerous enough just by itself.

Chapter 23

THE SECOND TRIP through the tunnels was easier because it was familiar to me now. I started a map and added to it as we went along. I also carried water. It took twenty-three minutes to reach the cache, though we could have done it in less time if we had to. The passage beyond the cache grew smaller again and I had to crawl on my hands and knees. I didn't like that very much. The soldiers had probably used these tunnels a lot. There was just one thing I was wondering about: what if they had booby-trapped the tunnels? What if there were tripwires attached to explosives? After all, they were at war when they were here. I started looking for tripwires.

The passage went up and around a few turns. There was only enough room for one person to pass. It was so hot. I was sweating a lot and Hollie was panting. This section was longer than the other ones. I was guessing it was fifty or sixty feet long. If we didn't reach an opening soon I was going to turn back. But we did.

We entered another cache. There were rifles, bottles and things, and this time there were barrels. How did they get barrels in here? They must have taken them apart and put them back together. That seemed like a heck of a lot of work, but there was no other way. There was something else in here. The walls were shiny and wet. Water was running in from somewhere. Maybe we were near the surface. I wished I knew. I sat down to think. A voice inside told me to go back now. This was far enough for one day. But what if we were almost at the surface? It would be a shame to stop now. I turned around to look at the hole we had just crawled out . . . and got a fright. There were six of them!

Don't panic, I told myself. There is no need to panic. Panicking never helps. It will be easy enough to find out which one is the right one. I shone the light on the floor to look for my footprints but didn't find anything. I went to the wall. The holes were all the same size. My gut feeling told me it was the one on the right, but how could I know for sure?

It occurred to me that I would recognize which was the right one if I backed into each one, then came out again. So, I tried it, but it didn't work. None of them felt familiar. Now

I was really sweating. I tried it again. I backed into each hole about ten feet, then crawled into the cache, stood up and waited for a feeling of familiarity, but nothing came. I sat down on the floor of the cavern and felt an icy shiver run through my body. The feeling of being lost kept rising in me and I had to force it down. "I am not lost. Even if I have to crawl through all six passageways I will eventually find the right one, so, see, there is no need to panic." Even so, I had to fight down the feeling.

I tried to take a deep breath, but you can't really do that in caves. The air is too heavy and sluggish. It won't fill up your lungs. There isn't enough oxygen in it. I was about to start crawling through the first hole when an idea jumped into my head. I pulled the tool bag off my shoulder, put it down and opened it. "Hollie. Go find Seaweed! Go find Seaweed!"

I shined the flashlight on his face, then pointed it towards the wall. He gave a little bark, took off and disappeared into the second hole from the right. I got up and followed him. I could hear him inside the tunnel even though he sounded very far away. I knew he wasn't. A few minutes later, I found him. He had stopped where the tunnel went down. "Good dog, Hollie." I picked him up and put him back in the bag, then continued through the passage. Twenty minutes later we were back at the sub.

I fed Hollie and gave him some fresh water. Then I made a pot of tea, sat on the floor by the observation window and ate a can of peaches. My grandfather's words were echoing through my head. "You think nothing bad's going to happen to you," he said. That bugged me. I didn't want to believe him. I thought of Mr. Chee and wondered if I should try to meditate before going into the tunnels again. Instead, I ate my peaches slowly and thoughtfully, and that was surprisingly soothing.

An hour later we were back in the cavern with the six holes. On the opposite wall was just one hole, and we went into it. I didn't know if it was my imagination or not but I thought I smelled a little fresh air. It was certainly damp. Maybe it was just the dampness I smelled. But Hollie smelled it too. His nose was twitching. I never really got a good look at his face in the tunnels because I didn't want to shine the light directly into his eyes. He was so tough. He never complained.

We crawled through the next tunnel. Then I was glad we did because it opened up more. I could almost stand. It looked as though the tunnel was dug by someone about half a foot shorter than me. This section was level too, which was a lot easier. I was getting the feeling we were close to the entrance. I wondered where it would be. Where would we come out? Would it be inside an old well, inside an old house, in the basement of a church or temple? Or would it come out in the middle of the jungle or on the side of a cliff? Wherever it was, I knew it would be well hidden. I was more curious about that than anything else.

And then, we hit a dead end. I couldn't believe it. There was a solid wall of rock right in front of us. There was nowhere to go but back. I was disappointed. Probably one of the other six tunnels was the right one out. But it was hard to believe that anyone would go to all this trouble just to create a diversion. I looked closely at the edges of the wall in front of us. Maybe it was only meant to look solid. Maybe there was a way through it.

On the top right corner there was a loose rock. I pulled on it, twisted it back and forth, pushed on it, pulled on it and it came out. Then I loosened the one beneath it, and the next one. Five rocks came out. The rest was solid. But now there was a hole. I stuck the flashlight through. The tunnel went up at a sharp angle but was very small. I didn't like it at all. I wouldn't even be able to crawl on my hands and knees; I would have to lie flat on my stomach and wiggle like a snake. That was too tight for me. Nobody could squeeze through there. It was too steep too. We'd have to go back. Rats.

I lowered the flashlight. Then I noticed something. There was a faint light at the top of the passage. I shut off the flashlight and shut my eyes for a second. It was so quiet. All I could hear was Hollie's panting. I opened my eyes and looked up. Yes, there was definitely a light at the top. I turned the flashlight on again.

"Hmmm. Hollie. Do you think we should try this?" He sneezed a little. He had cave dust in his nose. I decided to try it. We could just slide back down if we had to. I would talk to Hollie the whole way to keep us both calm. Then I realized that I had been talking to him the whole time already. I pushed him into the opening and climbed up after him. I forced him ahead a little at a time. It wasn't as difficult as I thought it would be; it was just really small. It was hard on the knees and elbows though. Because I was on my stomach I could only push with my toes and twist my body back and forth. It was really hot too, but the farther we went, the fresher the air became. That was really encouraging. Then we heard a strange noise, like a deep humming. The closer we came to the light, the louder the noise was. What the heck was that?

The tunnel came out in the most confusing way. But it was very smart. At the top it went up and backwards, like the top of a candy cane. It opened behind an edge of rock, and that was in the very top of the entrance to a much larger cave, a big open one. So, in a way, the entrance wasn't hidden at all, but at the same time you couldn't possibly see it. It was right in front of you if you were standing on the ground inside the cave, but you couldn't see it. From the ground the rock looked like one piece, but there was actually a tiny hole there that you could only see when you were almost in it. To get into it you had to raise yourself twelve feet off the ground. But there was nothing to hold on to, to climb up.

The humming noise was the wind. When we came to the end of the tunnel the wind was roaring like a jet engine. The typhoon had arrived.

Getting out was hard. I pushed Hollie through and held on to the tool bag strap. Then, I squeezed my body through, though the rock scraped my stomach and legs on the way out. It was a twelve-foot drop to the ground. I held on to Hollie and tried to climb partway down before dropping but it still knocked the wind out of me.

The cave was on the edge of a jungle. The wind was flattening the trees. The sky was black. I held Hollie against my stomach in the bag. The wind was grabbing at everything. There was shelter in the bigger cave but there was something I wanted to do. I wanted to find the ocean and identify where we were from the water.

I climbed the hill above the cave. It was hard to walk in the wind! It was so strong I knew it could pick us up and throw us, so I walked low and kept my hands close to plants to grab them and hold on if I had to. I had never seen wind like this before, not even at sea.

On the other side of the hill I saw the water. I stared at the hill's features and tried to memorize them. Then I climbed back down to the cave, turned right and followed the edge of the jungle for a few hundred feet. A path went down the hill into another big open cave. I figured this was the one with the people in it, that I had seen from the sub. A wooden sign on the ground said, "Grotto."

Getting back inside our cave was really difficult. I had to find a log to lean against the stone wall, climb up on it and pull myself up, which was really hard with my weak arm. If

I hadn't trained myself to do chin-ups I would never have been able to get up. There was almost nothing to hold on to. It looked as though the rock face didn't go anywhere, but just above the top was a little shadow behind a ridge, and beneath that shadow was the tiny hole, barely big enough to squeeze into. As I pulled myself up I kicked the log down and saw it roll into the cave. No one would ever guess why it was there. Probably they'd think the wind had blown it there. As I disappeared into the secret tunnel, pulling Hollie in after me, I had to grin at how clever the Japanese soldiers had been.

Chapter 24

WE SPENT TWO DAYS in the cavern. I kept one floodlight on when we were outside of the sub and had to pump fresh air into the sub from the tanks. The air of the cavern was stale and it never felt as though we could get quite enough oxygen. For the same reason I couldn't run the engine, so I pedalled the bike for a few hours each day to make up for the power we used. We slept, ate, exercised and relaxed. I read the entire *Rime of the Ancient Mariner* aloud to the crew. They were a good audience. Hollie kept his head on his paws the entire time and Seaweed kept one eye open, which meant he was either half asleep or half awake. I also practised diving.

It was seventy-five feet to the bottom. When I flicked on the underwater floodlights and looked down through the observation window I could see all the way, though the water was a little murky. The undercurrent was pulling water in and out of the tunnel that connected the cavern to the sea. The pull was not so strong as to affect the surface water inside the cavern but I'd have to be careful at the bottom not to get sucked into it.

Lighting up the cavern above and below the surface with floodlight, I slipped into the water, took several deep breaths and went down. The sides were smooth and perfectly round. The cavern must have been carved from millions of years of erosion. It was the perfect hiding place for a small submarine and a perfect place to practise free diving. For about two hours I went up and down, timing how long I was underwater. Two minutes and fifteen seconds was my longest, but I felt that after a few days here I could stretch that to two and a half minutes. It was the very best place to practise because there were no distractions, especially nothing to startle me. Well, almost nothing.

I was coming up very relaxed, had my eyes closed and was concentrating on Mr. Chee's words. It occurred to me that diving was probably similar to meditating because you sort of emptied your mind and had to relax, except that I wasn't sitting still on a floor, I was swimming underwater and was about forty-five seconds away from drowning if I didn't surface in time. Except for that, they were probably similar.

Then, my fingers touched something and I opened my eyes. Right in front of me was one of the skeletons drifting down slowly. I was face to face with it. I knew which one it was too—the funny one.

Fright went through me like a bullet and my air was suddenly used up. I started swimming up as quickly as I could, trying to stay calm on the way. How did the skeleton get in the water? Did it just fall? I didn't think so. Was there someone or something in the cave? Was I going to surface and find someone there?

I broke the surface and gasped for air. I turned and looked at the skeletons. Now there were just four. Standing on the card table, looking fed up with their company, was Seaweed. Suddenly he hopped onto the head of another of the soldiers and its head fell off, hit the ground and rolled into the water.

"Seaweed! Don't! Don't peck!"

Well, that settled that. I decided to give the soldiers a burial at sea. It wouldn't take long and it wouldn't be very ceremonial. I didn't know what to say so I carried my book over and read a verse from *The Rime of the Ancient Mariner* that seemed fitting to me.

> *Oh sleep! It is a gentle thing.*
> *Beloved from pole to pole!*
> *To Mary Queen the praise be given!*
> *She sent the gentle sleep from Heaven,*
> *That slid into my soul.*

I reached over to push each soldier into the water and watch it sink. But . . . I couldn't do it. I didn't know why. For the first time, perhaps because of the words of the poem, I felt more than fascination for the soldiers. I felt sad for them. Now I was unsure that this was the right thing to do. I stood and thought about it. Nope. It wasn't right. I didn't know what to do but I couldn't do this. Shoot! Now I had to swim back down and bring up the sunken skeleton and the other head too. Oh boy.

It took eleven dives! What a lot of work. It wouldn't have been so hard if all of the bones had stayed together. Some of the smaller bones of the hands and feet were missing but I decided not to worry about that. They were too hard to find even with the floodlights on. I just didn't count them. Getting the two skulls up was the trickiest part. I took potatoes out of a burlap sack and carried them up in that, along with some of the other loose bones. I piled everything on top of the card table and told Seaweed to leave it alone.

After two days I decided to check on the typhoon. I shut the hatch with Hollie and Seaweed inside, took the dinghy to the ledge and climbed into the passageway by myself. It was a lot easier alone and I even enjoyed it. I could see why some people enjoyed cave exploring the way I enjoyed free diving. Both required self-control, clear thinking and lots of physical energy. Both were personally rewarding.

As I approached the opening I realized there was no humming sound. The typhoon had passed. I wondered how much damage it had done. I stuck my head out but didn't bother climbing down. I wanted to go back and let Seaweed out so that he could fly. To do that, I would have to take the sub out into the sea.

So, I returned to the sub and we submerged and went through the narrow tunnel. The undertow pulled us against the rock a few times on our way out. When the periscope broke the surface I looked around. It was clear so I opened the hatch and Seaweed came right up, took a peek, then jumped into the air. He was one happy bird. Hollie and I went back into the cavern.

This time I packed a lunch, put it in a bag, put Hollie in the tool bag, took the camera and climbed through the passageway one more time. It was a lot to carry, but my confidence in knowing the way made it so much easier. Coming out of the final tunnel, I felt like toothpaste squeezing out of a tube. Then we jumped down into the sunshine of a brand new day.

It looked as though giants had stomped all over the island, crushing trees and leaving broken branches, roots and fruit everywhere. Saipan had coconuts, oranges, bananas, lemons, papaya, mangos, and a bunch of other fruits I had never seen before. And they were all over the ground. There were also puddles of water everywhere, as if a tsunami had rolled over the island, though no tsunami could reach so high. I followed the path that led down past the Grotto and onto a road that was well paved. The road wound like a coiled snake. I saw a sign that pointed uphill towards the "Suicide Cliffs," and downhill towards the city of Garapan. I let Hollie out and we started up.

It was extremely hot and humid. I was sweating a lot and Hollie was panting. But the sky was blue, the sun bright and the view very pleasant. We could see ocean all around. After a while I heard a bus coming from below. As it passed us I saw it was filled with Japanese tourists. Everyone waved and took our picture. I waved back and took a picture of the back of the bus as it coughed and wheezed its way up the hill. When we reached the top, I saw three more busses and a small crowd of tourists spread out among a handful of monuments near the edge of the cliffs. Most of the tourists were taking pictures but some were kneeling at the monuments and some of them were crying. I was surprised by that because the war had ended such a long time ago.

Hollie and I went to the edge of the cliff where there was a railing. If you climbed over it you would fall right off the cliff. I was a little nervous that Hollie might get too close to the edge but he was even more careful than I was. From where we stood we could see far across the Philippine Sea. We could see the green hills and jungle of the island, which from the distance didn't look affected by the typhoon at all, and we could see a dozen beautiful white birds, like doves, gliding around and around in a spiral below us. It was a beautiful view from the top of the Suicide Cliffs.

I tried to imagine people jumping from this spot, because this was where it had happened—a sign sticking out of the ground said so in several languages. The busloads of Japanese tourists said so, especially the people kneeling on the ground crying.

I tried to imagine it, jumping from here. I shut my eyes, opened them and looked down, shut them, opened them . . . no way! I could never do it in a million years. It would be impossible for me to jump. Nothing in the world could have made me. They would have had to shoot me; I would not have jumped.

But others had. I had read about it. Women and children, even women with babies, lined up in rows and jumped. They helped each other jump. They held hands and jumped together. I couldn't imagine it. There was something missing in my understanding. I had no idea what it was; I just knew there was something missing. Nothing here made any sense to me.

And then, almost as if he knew what I was thinking, a man who had been kneeling at the monuments came over to me and touched my shoulder. I turned and looked at him. He stared into my eyes and smiled, but it was a sad smile. He had been crying. I wasn't used to seeing a grown man cry. I felt awkward and wondered why he had come to me. He wanted to shake my hand, so I gave it to him and he shook it, all the while staring me in the eye. Then, he closed his eyes. But he was still holding my hand. It looked like he was praying. He said something to me in Japanese. I didn't know what to say back so I just said, "Thank you." He bowed, so I bowed back. Suddenly he let go of my hand and reached into his pocket for a notepad and pen. He drew a picture of a woman jumping off the cliff and showed it to me. I dropped my head. I didn't know what to say. Then he drew another picture. He sighed heavily and handed me the notepad. I took it and looked at it. It was a man sitting inside a cave.

I stared at the drawing. I wondered if his father had died in the caves. He said something to me in Japanese. It sounded like a question. But I couldn't take my eyes off the picture. He put his hand on mine again and said something and questioned me with his eyes. How could I tell him that I had just found five skeletons in a cave? How could I show him? I couldn't really. He was too old to climb through the caves, and I couldn't carry them out. Nor did I want to take them out with the sub. And yet it felt so wrong not to do something or say something. But what could I do?

He started to go. I had to think of something. I reached over and touched the arm of his jacket. He turned around very surprised. I pointed to the notepad and made the gesture of telephoning. Would he give me his phone number? He didn't understand and so I kept trying until he did. Finally he wrote down his phone number. Then he asked for mine so I wrote Ziegfried's. We shook hands again and he wandered back to the monument.

I took pictures from the edge of the cliff. I took pictures of the tourists, the monuments and buses, then we started back down the hill. Seaweed spotted us and joined us. Oddly, it felt as if we could have been walking down any road back home in Newfoundland on a hot summer's day. But we weren't. We were in Saipan. Things had happened here that were worse than my worst nightmares. But I didn't understand any of it.

And I wanted to.

Garapan, Saipan's only town, was four miles away. After a mile or so we began to see houses and shops, and the farther we went the more we saw. Everything was made of concrete, and I could understand why. Anything else would have blown away in the typhoons. Along the road we saw broken trees, branches and fruit strewn everywhere. I picked up two bananas and four oranges on the way and ate them. There were large crabs scurrying across the road too, as if they were lost and confused. Had the typhoon blown them so far from the beach? Or did they live in the jungle? Were these the coconut crabs that I had read about? There were so many of them. Hollie sniffed at them cautiously. Seaweed attacked and ate one. I didn't interfere. If I had, he would just have flown farther away and eaten another one. Seaweed didn't take orders from anyone when it concerned what went into his belly. How free it must have felt to be him, I thought. When you were a bird you never had to worry about war or suicide. All day you could just eat, sleep, and fly. I smiled. The longer I lived with Seaweed, the more I felt that birds were smarter than humans.

Chapter 25

THE CIRCUS SHIP looked like a worn-out traveller. She sat moored to the dock as if she had sailed in on her last breath and gone into a deep sleep. But I was excited to see her, more excited than I thought I would be. Across from the pier was a park. People were clearing broken trees and branches from the ground and setting up tents. The circus had come to town.

Hollie and I wandered over. I saw people from the ship. Then, I saw Cinnamon, and she saw me. She came running and I was pretty sure she left the ground before she hit me. Her arms were wide open and her hug knocked me off balance and we both landed on the ground.

"Alfred! You came! You really came!"

"Uhhh, yah. I said I would."

"But you did! You really did! I can't believe it. I'm so happy."

She jumped up, grabbed my arm and yanked me up. I was reminded how strong she was. Suddenly her face darkened. "You left without saying goodbye."

"You fell asleep! I asked Megara to say goodbye for me. And I told you I would meet you here."

She eyed me suspiciously. "You should have woken me."

"Sorry."

Her face brightened again. "It's okay. You're here now."

I looked around. "So, you survived the typhoon?"

"That was just a little one. They say a bigger one is coming next week. We're setting up really fast. Do you want to help?"

"Uhh, I suppose I could."

Cinnamon looked down at Hollie, and Hollie looked up at her, but she didn't bend down to pat him. "You'd better keep a close eye on your dog though. There are lots of boonie dogs in Saipan, and the locals eat dog."

"Oh. What's a boonie dog?"

"Just a stray dog. They're the dogs that are left behind when people move here for a few years then leave. They leave their pets behind. And they form packs. They bark at you a lot but they're actually really afraid of people. They know that people eat them here. They're really unfriendly to new dogs, especially little ones. Sometimes a boonie dog will wander onto the ship. Not a good idea. You know what happens then."

"Yup."

I spent the rest of the day helping the circus set up, which meant carrying poles, boxes, tables, tarps and staging across the dock to the park. Everything was pulled from the ship with a pulley system, swung around and lowered onto the dock. Hollie spent most of the day sleeping in the tool bag. Sometimes he was on my back and sometimes beside me on the ground but never out of my sight. When it turned dark we stopped to eat supper. Pierre had set up a barbecue and had grilled a fresh tuna with rice and served it to everyone who helped. It was the best thing I ever tasted. After we finished, Cinnamon said she was free to take a walk with me.

We strolled along the road and the beach. Hollie walked close to my heels. He always sensed my caution and imitated it. The road was littered with branches and the beach was covered with rocks, shells and seaweed thrown up from the typhoon. I asked Cinnamon if she had been frightened by it.

"Not at all. I've seen lots of typhoons. And bigger than this one."

"What will you do if a bigger one comes?"

"We'll stay here in the lagoon. That's the safest place for a ship. What will you do, stay on the bottom of the sea? I want to go in your submarine again."

"Actually, I found a cave where I am keeping it."

"Really? You found a cave for your submarine?"

"Yah. It's really hidden. Nobody would ever find it in a million years. It has skeletons in it."

She stopped. "Skeletons?"

I nodded. "From the war."

"Weren't you afraid?"

"No."

"Why not?"

"I don't know. You get used to that, I guess. I'm pretty used to it now."

She shook her head. "How do you get used to skeletons?"

"I don't know, you just do. Living things are scarier than dead things when you think about it."

"They are?"

"Yes."

"Hmmm. I don't know about that."

"They are. Trust me."

We walked in silence. There were small concrete pavilions on the beach. As we passed one, Cinnamon pointed to an old man sitting there staring out at the sea. He was surrounded by dogs. "He was in the war."

"How do you know?"

"Everyone knows. He's crazy. They say he was here as a young man during the fighting and that he never left. Now he's an old man and he collects boonie dogs."

"Does he eat them?"

"I don't think so."

I counted thirteen dogs as we passed. They were big and small, though none as small as Hollie. Hollie eyed them nervously but the dogs stayed with the old man. I tried to take a closer look at him but he kept his head down. He was wearing very old, faded military fatigues and his hair was long, grey and stringy. He looked like a hobo but the dogs seemed to love him. I was curious. "Do you think we could talk to him?"

"No way! He's crazy!"

"How do you know he's crazy?"

"Everyone says that. And look at him. He talks to himself all the time. And who would stay around after a war for the rest of his life? You'd have to be crazy."

"I suppose."

I thought of the soldiers in the cave. They never had a choice.

After our walk, I said goodnight to Cinnamon at the ship. She asked me where I was going to sleep.

"I don't know. Somewhere."

"In a cave with skeletons?"

"Not tonight. Maybe on the beach."

"You're coming back tomorrow, right?"

"I am."

"Do you promise?"

I nodded. I didn't know why she liked me so much, but I didn't mind.

Long after darkness had fallen and Cinnamon went inside

the ship, I was still wandering along the beach, slowly sifting my feet through the warm sand. It was still hot out, and I loved that. Hollie still had lots of energy, which was amazing. He never wasted opportunities to run around on land. He ran back and forth between the water and me, sniffing everything. Seaweed dropped by for a while, then disappeared again. Eventually I sat down and stared at the moon. The sand was soft and comfortable. I wondered how to tell the Japanese man about the skeletons. Could one of them have been his father? Imagine! I really had to do something.

I sat until I got sleepy, then spread my jacket beneath me, lay down and went to sleep. Hollie curled up beside me. I heard him snort sand out of his nose as I drifted off.

In the morning I raised my head and saw the old man. He was down at the edge of the water, surrounded by his pack of dogs. Maybe he had seen me, but he was ignoring me. I was curious. Would it be so bad if I talked to him? So what if he was crazy? I could just walk away.

Cinnamon was right, he was talking to himself. But he stopped when I approached. He must have been surprised to see someone coming towards him. He raised his head but didn't look at me. I couldn't tell if he was crazy or not. "Good morning."

He looked uncertain. He was struggling to speak. "Mornin.'"

He had a deep voice and a heavy accent that was probably from the American south. I decided to come right out and ask him what I wanted to know. Why not? "I was told that you served in the war here."

His eyebrows lifted up and he turned and looked at me as if he were staring at a ghost. "Suppose."

"And . . . I heard that you've never left the island since then. Is that true?"

His eyes went into a stare and they went far away. He didn't answer. Slowly, he came closer. His eyes focused on Hollie in my arms. Then he looked at me as clear as day. "Would you like some coffee?"

Chapter 26

HIS NAME WAS Paul Lafayette. He was from New Orleans. I walked with him to his tiny concrete house across the road, opposite the beach. It was almost hidden beneath coconut trees, lemon trees and bushes. The back half of the house was open, just a roof covering a table and an open kitchen. There were hundreds of yellow butterflies in the bushes. I smiled when I saw them.

The dogs came in and settled on the floor. I had put Hollie inside the tool bag but Paul said not to worry; the dogs would not hurt him. He was right. When I let Hollie out, they treated him like a friend. There was a lot of butterfly flapping and dog-tail wagging in Paul's kitchen.

"We don't see too many visitors," he said. "In fact, you're the first one in about ten years."

"Why do you have so many dogs?"

He filled the kettle and put it on the stove. "Most abandoned dogs join the packs. These are the ones that were rejected. They usually end up on the beach. Sooner or later they find their way to me."

He toasted two whole loaves of bread on the grill, buttered them and shared them with the dogs and me. He served me a cup of very strong coffee and sat down. He held his cup in two hands, blew across the top and started to talk. It sounded like a confession, as if he had been waiting a long time to tell it. I listened in utter fascination as he told me how he came to the Pacific as a young man on board a navy ship. He was a marine. Climbing into the landing barge to take Saipan was his first taste of combat.

"The fighting was so vicious. Nothing in training, nothing in the world prepared us for it. We outnumbered them more than two to one. We had better weapons, more ammunition and better air-cover. For every American soldier who died, ten Japanese soldiers were killed. But still, they wouldn't quit. No matter what we did they wouldn't surrender. We killed a thousand of them every day for a month. It just didn't stop. And then . . ."

"And then?"

Paul went into a blank stare again. He didn't look sad or anything, just very far away. "And then they started jumping from the cliffs, the women and children."

"I was up there, yesterday. I couldn't understand how anybody could jump."

"Well, they did." He paused. "And they hid in the caves."

"I know. I found one."

"There are caves all over this island. We linked arms, five thousand of us, and walked every inch of the island, and still we couldn't find them. They kept up a guerrilla campaign even after we had taken the island. Nothing, *nothing* would make them quit."

"But eventually they did. They must have."

He shook his head. "No. We sealed up some of the caves, locking them inside. And ... we brought out flame throwers."

He stopped. I waited. He reached down and scratched the head of an old dog. "There's a library here, Alfred. Have you been to it?"

"No, I just got here."

"You should go. They have real film footage of the battle. You can see it. You can see everything."

"I'd love to do that. I will."

He looked at me strangely, almost suspiciously. "Well, you can see it, yes. You can see it all."

"Even people jumping from the cliffs?"

"Everything."

He stopped, dropped his head low and ran his fingers through his stringy grey hair. Suddenly he raised his head and looked at me again. "I put myself under house arrest, you understand?"

"What?"

"Nobody ordered me to. I just decided after what I had done I would confine myself to house arrest for the rest of my life."

"So it's true? You never left?"

"It's true. Except for crossing the road to the beach for the dogs and going to the store, I never leave this house."

"You haven't left since the end of the war?"

"No. This is my third house on this spot. The first two were destroyed by typhoons. The typhoons are getting worse, you know. It's global warming. We don't deserve this planet."

"But . . . what did you do that was so bad?"

He raised his thumb and bit the nail. "When you watch those films . . ."

"Yes?"

"You'll see the flame-throwers."

"Okay?"

"You'll see women coming out of the caves. You'll see babies in their arms."

"Oh."

"We burnt them."

I realized I had stopped breathing. "You were a flame-thrower?"

He dropped his head and nodded. I felt like I couldn't breathe.

"Do you want some more coffee?"

"Uhh . . . I don't know."

I couldn't think. I was feeling sick in my stomach. Paul

reached over and filled my cup with coffee. Then he sat back and stared at a butterfly that landed on his shoulder. I needed to see the films at the library. I had to.

"Will you come back and visit me again?"

"Sure."

There was nothing about Paul that looked criminal, that was for sure. He was probably the gentlest man I had ever met. I felt sorry for him. I couldn't understand why he couldn't forgive himself.

Two hours later I was sitting in a tiny projection room in the Saipan Public Library, a long concrete bunker that could have been any library in any town in North America. The film I was watching was in black and white. It showed the American ships arriving and shelling the island and soldiers climbing into the landing barges and jumping onto the beach. Jeeps landed, tanks landed, airplanes flew overhead and dropped bombs. Everywhere there were explosions, smoke and confusion. I couldn't believe it was the same island, and yet I recognized it. Then I saw the cliffs. It looked like things were falling off. But the camera went closer and I saw people, big ones and small ones. They were dropping down to the ground, though some were hitting the rocks on the way. Some were waving their arms and screaming. Some just fell silently. I was horrified.

Then I saw soldiers at the entrance to caves. Some of the caves were just small holes in the ground. The soldiers were smiling as they pointed to them. I tried to see the faces of the soldiers. Sometimes they were smiling for the camera. Sometimes they weren't. They had discovered Japanese soldiers hiding. Now they were leading them in a row with their hands on top of their heads. The Japanese soldiers were very small. They were in bare feet and their clothes were just rags.

Then I saw soldiers with tanks on their backs. They shot fire from them and I could not believe how far the flames reached. They must have sprayed a hundred feet. And then I saw soldiers standing by the entrance to a cave. I looked to see if I could recognize Paul. He was just a young man then, just a couple of years older than me. I didn't recognize him. The soldiers must have suspected the enemy was hiding in the cave. They shot flames inside. Women came running out, and they were carrying babies and they were on fire. They burned to death right there. I dropped my head. What was I doing? What was I watching? Why was I here? Suddenly I wished I hadn't seen it. I wanted to take it away. I wanted to go back to where I was before I had watched that film.

But I couldn't.

Chapter 27

I WANDERED AWAY from the library very slowly with Hollie on my back. There was a Japanese garden nearby and we went in there. It was full of butterflies too. What I couldn't understand, and couldn't believe, was that these were human beings, both the ones coming out of the caves on fire and the ones throwing flames at them. They were humans. I was human. We were the same. Why was it happening? How could things go so terribly wrong?

I knew it was war. I understood that. Japan had attacked America. America fought back. But those were just countries, just names. I could understand when I thought of countries fighting countries the way I read in books. I could not understand when it was people, like the man on the cliff who had shaken my hand. Like Paul. These were real people I had met. They had been enemies. Both sides fought and killed each other here, in this place that was now so beautiful and peaceful. It was insane.

I understood Paul's imprisonment better now, even though it still didn't feel right. He didn't start the war. He didn't invent flame-throwers. If I had stood in his place back then with a flame-thrower on my back, would I have turned it on women and children? No. I knew that I wouldn't have. I was certain of that. I would have jumped from the cliffs before I would have burned people alive. But, I hadn't been here then. Paul had. And he had done it. Was I so different from him? I didn't think so. I just knew I couldn't do what he had done. And I didn't want to think about it anymore. But I couldn't stop. Sheba was right. Well, she was right and she wasn't. I wanted to know and I didn't.

I let Hollie out and we wandered until we found ourselves back at the circus ship. The park was filled with people now. The circus was opening soon. There were so many people—I was amazed. According to my guidebook, about ninety thousand people lived on Saipan, sixty thousand of them coming from other countries. But they were spread out across the island so there didn't seem to be so many. This was the most people I had seen gathered in one place in a long time.

The crowd was excited. There were smells of barbecues

and popcorn and cotton candy in the air. The smells tugged at me. I wanted to enjoy them but I felt torn inside. Part of me didn't want to let go of the heavy thoughts. Part of me wanted to forget them altogether.

And I had always wanted to see a circus.

The old grey tents were covered with colourful ribbons. Ticket booths were set up and people were lined up at them. I saw signs advertising various acts: a wild elephant and two ferocious lions; Medusa, the snake lady who would turn you to stone if you stared into her eyes; the original wolf man, who had to be kept in a cage; the incredible family of flying trapeze artists who defied gravity; and Hugo, the strongest man in the world. The opening act would feature Dickie, the funniest clown the world has ever known. I didn't remember Cinnamon telling me about a clown. I wondered who he was.

As I stood at the edge of the park and watched, still unsure whether or not to go in, I saw something that made me feel better. Standing in line for tickets were people from different countries: America, Japan, China, the Philippines, as well as the local people, the Chamorro. They were all talking and laughing. They were excited. A couple of generations ago they were killing each other here. Now, they were lining up to enjoy a circus. Before I could think another thought, Cinnamon came out of one of the tents, spotted me and rushed over. "Alfred! Oh! I am so glad you are here. I was afraid you weren't coming."

"I promised you I would."

"I know, but people make promises they don't keep."

"I keep mine."

She broke into a smile, leaned over and kissed me on the cheek. I blushed.

"You can come into the tent and watch the show. You don't have to pay because you helped set up. I'm not on for a couple of hours. Dickie is first."

"Who's Dickie?"

"The clown."

"I know, but who is he?"

She grinned. "You'll see. I'm so happy you are here." She took me to an entrance at the back of the tent and hurried off. I watched her bounce across the grass like a gazelle.

I went inside and took a seat on the rickety old wooden grandstand. I had seen them folded up on the ship. I was the first and only one seated. As I looked around I was amazed at how big the tent seemed from the inside. It was hard not to feel excited. What was it about a circus, even a little one like this, that was so special?

But I was a little nervous for Cinnamon. What if she became distracted and made a mistake and injured herself? I didn't even really understand why she liked me so much in the first place, except that, like me, she didn't have any friends her own age. I supposed that was it. I had Hollie and Seaweed. She only had snakes.

The main flap opened and people started to pour in. Loud

recorded music started playing at the same time. It was old fashioned music yet it made me laugh with anticipation. I couldn't help it. The people coming in were excited too. They must have seen this circus before, when the ship had visited in other years, yet they flocked in and crowded together on the seats as if everything were brand new. I hoped the old wooden grandstands would hold up. Suddenly there were people all around me, even pressed up against my shoulders. I put the tool bag on my lap and Hollie stood up and watched through the mesh.

When the tent was filled with people, the music didn't seem so loud anymore. There was a deep hum of people talking, laughing and whistling so loudly I almost covered my ears. Suddenly the Master of Ceremonies appeared and the noise level rose even higher. I looked around me. People were going crazy and the show hadn't even started yet. The MC was dressed in a dazzling red, white and blue costume covered in jewels. When he opened his mouth and started speaking I couldn't believe this was the same quiet man I had seen on the ship. His voice boomed across the tent and everyone shut up and listened. He told us we were in for the most thrilling circus night imaginable. Something about the way he said it made me think it was true. He described all the acts that were coming but said we had to watch the funniest clown in the world first because immediately after his act he was going to retire. Everyone groaned sadly. The moment he retired, the MC continued, he was going to fly to the moon. In fact, he was going to fly from this very tent, tonight! The audience roared again.

"And now!" roared the MC, "a big round of applause for Dickie! The funniest clown in the worrrrrrrrrrrrld!"

The people in the audience whistled, cheered and stomped their feet. It was deafening. A flap opened at one end of the tent and a small clown wandered in slowly, looking lost and unsure of himself. The music stopped. The crowd grew silent. The clown shuffled slowly and sadly to the centre of the ring. He plopped down on the ground and began crying. I thought that was very strange and wasn't sure it was an act. I looked around and saw that everyone was still smiling. The clown kept crying. He was wiping his eyes with his sleeves and crying harder all the time. I was trying very hard not to feel sorry for him—he was, after all, a clown in a circus—but I couldn't help it. Then, as if he suddenly realized something, he lifted his foot up so that everyone could see it, and he pointed to it. He raised his head in a gesture, asking the crowd a question. Everyone in the tent roared, "Yes!" Then he started to pull a tack from his foot. But the tack was attached to a coloured scarf and the scarf kept coming out until it was about twenty feet long. The audience burst with laughter. The clown sprang to his feet and started to run around in a circle. He was fast! Then he stopped, all out of breath. And then, he started to laugh. He started with a giggle that turned into a chuckle that turned into a belly laugh. He laughed and laughed with the funniest laugh I ever heard and he didn't stop. The audience laughed hysterically with him. And now I knew who he was, because I recognized his laugh. Dickie the Clown was Mr. Chee.

After Dickie the Clown, we were treated to the frightening spectacle of three wild beasts rolled into the centre of the ring inside two cages: two lions in one, and the wolf man in the other. One of the lions was so dangerous it was not allowed out, said the MC. Although I remembered something about it being too old, I really wasn't sure—the MC was so convincing. The really frightening thing was that the wolf man was chained and locked up, but he escaped! And he was scary. He went around frightening everyone, and the lion tamer had to use one of the lions to chase him back into his cage. It really made me nervous. I was so caught up in the action I completely forgot I had met these people before.

And then the lights dimmed and Medusa appeared. She was wearing snakes all over her body. The audience was warned not to look directly into her eyes or they would be turned to stone. Around and around the circle Medusa wandered, trying to get the audience to stare at her. People in the front rows screamed. People in the back laughed hysterically. I had thought Megara was scary enough with the snakes in her room. Now she was wearing something that made her eyes shine like floodlights. It was very frightening.

Next, Dickie the Clown returned riding Mindy, the elephant. He was standing on her back and bouncing up and down out of rhythm with her stride. He fell off twice and climbed back up. They went around the circle a few times and back out. I was laughing so hard my eyes were running with tears.

We had a brief intermission while a giant net was carried in and tied to the poles about ten feet off the ground. A large flap opened up and two giants stepped into the ring. They were walking on enormously high stilts and wearing giant papier-mâché heads. They were amazing. The giants played with yo-yos ten feet long!

Finally, the MC returned and told the audience in a very serious tone that the acrobats were about to try a new routine that had never been successfully performed before. In fact, it was so dangerous that an unmentionable number of people had died trying to do it. Then, he asked the audience to be as quiet as they possibly could while the artists were in the air, and to save their applause for when the performers were back on their perch. I looked around and saw heads nodding in agreement everywhere. I hoped everyone was paying attention. A drum roll began. The older couple appeared in their sleek and colourful suits. And then I saw Cinnamon appear. She looked so wonderful and I realized that, once again, Sheba had been right—I had met someone very special.

Chapter 28

THE FLYING-TRAPEZE act was a huge hit. Cinnamon flew through the air as if she had wings. It was incredible. I needn't have worried. Nobody missed their connections. Nobody fell. They spun somersaults through the air and grabbed each other's hands without even looking. I didn't know if it was the most difficult act in the world but it sure was exciting.

There were a few more acts after that. Then Dickie the Clown returned to say farewell and fly to the moon. He went around shaking hands with everyone in the front row. Everyone wanted to touch his hand. He burst out crying again; he couldn't help it. Everyone felt sad. A cannon was rolled into the tent. Blowing kisses with both hands, Dickie climbed into the cannon backwards, waved one last time and disappeared inside the barrel. There was a long drum roll. I didn't dare blink. Then there was an explosion and smoke filled the centre of the tent. It smelled like firecrackers. When it finally started to clear, the giants were standing in the centre. They pointed up to a hole in the roof of the tent. Dickie was gone. The giants waved to the moon. Everyone waved and cheered. I couldn't stop laughing. I had never had so much fun.

I met Cinnamon after the show. She had changed and was ready for a walk.

"Did you like it?"

"I loved it."

"Really?"

"It was great. I was amazed. You were really good."

"Did you think so? Thank you, Alfred. I'm so glad you saw it. And now you know who Dickie the Clown is."

"He's hilarious! I can't believe it."

We walked along the beach. Cinnamon took my hand. I didn't mind. We walked quietly for a while, but I could sense she wanted to say something.

"Alfred?"

"Yes."

"You should join our circus."

"What? Me? Join the circus?"

"Join *our* circus."

"But . . . what would *I* do? I can't do anything."

"Yes, you can. You can learn. You can learn to do anything. I didn't know anything when I joined."

"But I'm an explorer. I have a submarine."

"I know. You can still keep your submarine."

I was so surprised. I never expected her to say that. We walked in silence again.

"I don't think so, Cinnamon. I belong on the sea. I'm a sailor."

"We're on the sea too! We're all sailors. We're a sailing circus. That's why you would fit in perfectly."

"I know, but it's not the same. I travel all over the world."

She moved closer and held my arm. "Is that your sore arm?"

"Yes, but it's getting a lot better."

"There's something else I want to ask you."

"What?"

She took a deep breath. "Don't answer right away, okay? Just think about it first."

"Okay."

"Will you think about it first?"

"Yes. I will. What is it?"

"Will you take me to Goa in your submarine so that I can look for my brother, and then take us back?"

Whoa. I never expected her to ask me that either. "Take you all the way to India?"

"And back. Don't answer yet . . . unless your answer is yes."

I dropped my head. There wasn't anything for me to think about. I knew the answer was no. But I didn't want to say it and she didn't want to hear it. So, we walked quietly again. I felt bad about it but I just knew it wasn't a good idea.

"Are you thinking about it?"

"Yes."

"Do you know what your answer is?"

"Yes."

"And?"

"I'm sorry, Cinnamon. It isn't a good idea. It's very small inside my submarine, and India is far away. It's dangerous and I can't protect you."

"You don't have to protect me."

"If you come inside my submarine, yes, I do. I'm the captain and that makes it my responsibility."

"You don't have to be so strict about it."

Actually, I did. I looked down at the gunshot wound on my arm. Then I thought of all the close calls we had had since going to sea. Just a few months earlier we had given a ride to a girl on the St. Lawrence River, and she had panicked when we got stuck on a cable sticking out of the *Empress of Ireland*, a huge luxury liner on the bottom of the river. When the girl panicked, I had to lie to her to calm her down. That was awful. I promised myself then that I would never take passengers again, except in emergencies, because I knew I couldn't really protect them. "I'm sorry."

Her face fell. "It's okay. I guess I knew that's what you would say. But you like me, right? We're friends, right?"

"Yes! I really like you a lot, I do. And I'm happy that we are friends."

"Well, *that's* good."

She squeezed my arm (it hurt, but I didn't say anything) and we continued our walk in silence.

I watched the circus the next night and the night after that. I enjoyed it more each time. It didn't matter when you knew what was going to happen; it was still exciting and funny. I sat closer to the front each night. When the giants came out they always scared me. When Dickie the Clown laughed, I laughed harder. When he cried and said he was leaving, I really felt sad, even though I knew it was all pretend. The circus was magic, it really was, and it swept me up in its spell. If I hadn't been so committed to exploring already I might really have considered joining them, though I couldn't imagine what I'd do. Maybe I would just sell tickets and popcorn and help set up and take down. But could I give up exploring the world to sell tickets and popcorn? No way. Besides, I really wanted to become an environmentalist now too. I didn't know how to do that exactly, but I would find out.

In the daytime between performances, Hollie and I explored Saipan. We walked up Mount Tapotchau, the highest point on the island, from where we could see Tinian, the island where the atomic bomb was kept before it was dropped on Japan. And we walked through jungle and down to some of the beaches. For a small island Saipan had a lot of interesting things to look at.

Hollie was happy with all the walking. So was I, but I was distracted too. No matter what we saw or what I thought about, my mind kept drifting back to Paul. It bothered me that he was stuck inside most of the time, that he never saw anyone but the dogs he rescued, that he couldn't forgive himself for something he had done such a long, long time ago. That didn't feel right. Even criminals who went to prison for murder were freed eventually. Why couldn't Paul be? I wanted to ask him that. I decided to visit him again.

It took an hour and a half to reach his house. It was easy to spot because of the yellow butterflies that hovered around it like yellow snowflakes. I went to the back and knocked.

A couple of dogs yipped inside. I could tell they were trying not to bark but couldn't help it; it was their nature. Paul came to the door and opened it cautiously. "Ahhh, Alfred, my friend. Come in. Coffee?"

I liked that he called me his friend. "Yes, please. Thank you."

"I didn't expect to see you again so soon. Did you visit the library?"

"Yes, I did."

I could tell by the look on his face that it really mattered to him whether I had or not.

"And you've come back to see me again?"

"Yes. I wanted to ask you something."

"Only one thing? I would expect a young man like you would have a whole lot of questions for a crazy old man like me."

That was true. I could have asked him questions all night long. "Yes, but there's one question in particular I'd like to ask you. If I don't, I think it will haunt me."

"Well, I can relate to that."

"Do you believe in ghosts? That's not my question. I'm just wondering if you do."

"Yes, I do. It doesn't matter if you believe in them or not. They're real."

"Do you see them?"

"Yes. I see the ghosts of the people I killed."

He poured boiling water into the percolator. The smell of coffee filled the little house. He was an old man but I kept thinking of him as a young man because he was young when he came here, and something about him felt as if time had stopped. It hadn't though; he was definitely old. He sat down again and stared across the table at me and waited patiently for me to ask my question.

It wasn't easy. "Do you think . . . do you think you will ever forgive yourself?"

He shut his eyes and slowly opened them. They were soft. They had the softness of someone who had been wounded, like a dog. He shut them again and dropped his head. A single word dropped out of his mouth. "No."

"But . . . why not? It was so long ago."

"Was it?" He got up and brought the coffee to the table. "Seems like yesterday to me."

"Really?"

"Have you ever killed anybody, Alfred?"

"No."

"Of course not. That would make you a murderer."

"But you didn't start the war."

"No. But I could have cleaned bedpans. I could have been a nurse. I could have nursed burn victims back to health instead of creating them. But I didn't. I wanted to be part of the action."

He stared intensely at me. "Sentencing myself to stay here until the day I die, on the very soil on which I killed innocent people, is the only way I can live with myself. And I have had to live with myself, you see, because I can never take another life, not even my own. I don't expect you to understand that."

"I guess I don't. I have to think about it. And I will. Thank you for answering my question."

"You're welcome."

He poured the coffee and we drank it. We didn't talk about the war anymore. We talked about the island and the sea. He asked me about my sub and journeys. He said Newfoundland sounded like a fascinating place because it was so far away. I laughed at that and assured him it wasn't. He said that if I had been born and raised on Saipan, Newfoundland would sound very exotic to me. But it didn't have typhoons, tsunamis, volcanoes, nuclear explosions or world wars, I said, just lots of fishing villages and fog. He said it sounded like heaven. That made me laugh.

When I was leaving, we shook hands at the door. There was no strength in his grip. I was used to strong handshakes—from Ziegfreid, my grandfather, and pretty much everyone else I met in Newfoundland, or on the sea. Paul's grip felt like the hand of a man who had given up on life a long time ago. Hollie and I went out. As we passed the window, I saw him return to the stove and drop his head. I felt a pain in my heart at the sight of it. And then, a wild idea jumped into my head and I went back to the door and knocked.

"Alfred? Did you forget something?"

"I have just one more question."

"Okay. Go ahead."

He braced himself.

"Will you come to the circus with me this evening? It starts in an hour. We'd have to leave now."

He stood there and just stared at me for the longest time, his eyes open wide. I was trying to think of something to say to convince him to come but I couldn't find the words. He surprised me. "Let me grab my jacket."

Chapter 29

SITTING WITH PAUL in the grandstands, waiting for the circus to begin, was the weirdest feeling. I felt honoured that he had come, that he trusted me enough to break his life-long sentence. But when the people crowded in and took their seats, no one sat directly beside us, as if we had leprosy or something. I supposed many of them recognized him and were afraid of sitting too close to a "crazy" person. And he did look like a hobo that had just wandered in. He didn't seem bothered by that though. He just sat calmly and without much expression. I wondered if seeing so many people so close might bother him but he hardly seemed to notice. He appeared unmoved by the excitement in the air.

When the MC came out, I felt the same excitement as before but I couldn't help stealing glances at Paul. Would the circus work its magic on him, as it did on everyone else?

If it did, he didn't show it. I was certain that when Dickie the Clown came out, Paul would start to laugh. But he must have been the only person in the whole tent who didn't. While people all around us were laughing, including me, Paul's eyes began to water. But he wasn't laughing.

It didn't look like he was crying either, although tears ran down his cheeks. His eyes were lit up and he definitely seemed interested in what we were watching, but he sat expressionless while the tears made two wet lines down the front of his face. How I wished I knew what he was thinking. But I didn't dare ask.

During the intermission I asked him if he would like some popcorn, and he nodded, so I stood in line and brought back a bag and we shared it. I saw people staring, pointing and talking about him, but nobody dared speak to him. That didn't surprise me. They would have if they had known how nice he really was.

Paul ate the popcorn the same way he watched the circus—without expression. I was beginning to wonder if I had been wrong, that the circus wouldn't affect him in a good way. But that wasn't so. When the show was over and we followed everyone outside, I asked him what he thought of it. He took my hands in his just the way Sheba did and looked into my eyes intensely. "That was the best thing I ever saw, Alfred. I just loved it. Is it on tomorrow too?"

"Yes, they're performing all week."

"Do you think we could go again?"

"Sure! I'd love to. Do you want me to come by your house at the same time tomorrow?"

"That would be great. Thank you, Alfred. Thank you so very much."

He shook my hands, let go, and wandered away. As I watched him go I thought how he looked like a young man and an old one at the same time, and that reminded me of Sheba too. How I wished he could have visited her. If anyone could help Paul with his past, it was Sheba.

After Paul had gone, Cinnamon came out and we went for our walk. I told her all about Paul. She listened carefully but she didn't understand why I wanted to get to know him or visit him, or especially why I wanted him to see the circus. And I didn't know how to explain it all to her.

"Making people laugh helps heal them from their injuries."

"But what injuries does he have?"

"In his heart."

"I don't understand. He's crazy!"

"No, he's not."

I could tell that she didn't understand, which surprised me. I thought that she would have.

The next night, I saw Paul smile. It was just a little smile, and it didn't come until near the end, when Dickie the Clown flew to the moon, but it was a real smile and it was like magic, as if a whole field of flowers blossomed in an instant. I never knew that such a small thing as a smile on an old man could look so wonderful.

When we came out of the tent that night, the winds had grown a lot stronger and there was a wild energy in the air. I found it exciting but people hurried home to board up their houses. The big typhoon was finally coming.

Paul said goodnight and went home too. I asked Cinnamon if she wanted to take a walk.

"I can't. We have to take the tents down tonight."

"Tonight? You're going to take them down right now?"

She frowned. "We have to. The typhoon will destroy them. Are you going to stay and help?"

"Of course."

We brought the animals back to the ship first. Then we pulled everything out of the tents and took the tents down. When things were brought onto the ship they had to be tied down. I couldn't believe how quickly conditions worsened. I also couldn't believe how fast everyone worked. They had obviously done this before.

It took all night. But we didn't see the sun when it came up. The darkness of night was replaced by the darkness of the storm. The sea tossed violently now, even in the lagoon. I couldn't imagine what the open sea was like. Everyone was exhausted. I sat down on the deck, where Cinnamon found me.

"Are you staying with us? We stay on the ship; it's safe inside the lagoon."

"I can't. I have to find Seaweed."

"Seaweed?"

"My first mate. He's a seagull."

I suddenly realized I hadn't seen Seaweed in over a day. I wondered if he had gone back to the spot where we had submerged the sub. That's what he would normally do when a storm was coming. Suddenly I was anxious to find him.

"Can I come?"

I looked at her. I wanted her to come. But I thought of the caves and how dark it was and how scary it would be to crawl through the top part for the first time. Even though she was so strong, what if she felt claustrophobic inside the cave? What would I do? What if she panicked? Would I be able to pull her through? I also had to carry Hollie. I wanted her to come, I really did, but I couldn't imagine it. I shook my head. "I'm sorry, Cinnamon. I want you to, I really do, but the caves are too dangerous. I will come back as soon as the typhoon is over. I promise."

She sighed and frowned. "I wish you weren't so afraid of me getting hurt. I'm not made of glass, you know."

"I know. I'm sorry. It's a promise I made to myself. I have to keep it."

Chapter 30

IT WAS A CRAZY race across the island; a race against the typhoon. I walked as quickly as I could and Hollie ran beside me. But when we left the shelter of trees and crossed the open spaces, I had to carry him in the tool bag. A couple of times—when the wind came sweeping down the road, carrying leaves and branches with it—I was barely able to stay on my feet. It was dangerous now. I had to watch carefully. Seaweed would not be in the air in this, he would be buckled down between some rocks for shelter. He was a very smart seagull, but I still worried about him. He would wonder where we were. I should have come back sooner.

I ran along the edge of the jungle until I reached the

Grotto, then up the hill to our cave. I ducked inside the open cavern, caught my breath and tried to think things through clearly. It would take at least an hour to climb through the caves with Hollie, jump into the sub and come up for Seaweed. And it was going to be a rough ride in the undertow now. But what if Seaweed wasn't there? I was assuming he was because that was his nature, but what if he wasn't? It would take me a whole hour to find out. The typhoon was getting worse every minute. I decided to climb over the hill and see if he was there first.

Something told me this typhoon was going to be a lot worse than the last one. I saw bunches of coconuts flying straight across the sky above me. Any wind that could do that could pick me up too. I bent low and held on to the rock as I scampered over the hill. The sea was wild but wasn't showing the full force of the typhoon on this side of the island yet. The sea was always a couple of hours behind the wind.

I climbed down the hill and found my first mate tucked in between two rocks. It was a good shelter from the wind but too close to the water for my liking. I had no doubt that the waves would grow and strike this very spot without warning. As smart and tough as he was, Seaweed had no experience with typhoons.

He squawked when he saw us, though I couldn't hear him above the wind. I'm sure he was glad to see us. I jumped down into the hollow and looked around. Could we sit out the typhoon here? Not a chance. The tide was out. This whole area would be under water in a few hours when the tide came in, not to mention the wrath of the winds. I stood up, looked down at the water tossing around like a pot boiling over on the stove, and I made a decision. Sometimes a desperate situation requires a desperate action.

I pulled the tool bag off and laid Hollie down beside Seaweed. They were both safe for the moment, tucked in away from the wind. The rain hadn't started yet, though it would soon. "Stay, Hollie!" I said, though I opened the hatch of the bag. I couldn't leave him locked in. What if I didn't make it back? He would have a chance to make it to the cave. But Seaweed wouldn't. No bird could fly in this wind. "Stay!" I said to them both. "I'll be right back."

I climbed down the rock, took several deep breaths and tried to calm myself. Mr. Chee's advice to meditate and live less dangerously flashed through my mind and I couldn't help but grin nervously. I took one last deep breath and dove into the sea.

I went straight down. The water was murky and pulled at me in every direction but I swam as strongly as I could without working too hard. I needed all the air that I had.

It was seventy-five feet down but it took longer than it should have because the undertow pulled me back and forth. At one moment it dragged me sideways so far that I thought I'd have to give up the idea. But it swung me back again and I kept going. At the bottom I saw the dim light of the Grotto cavern coming through its tunnel. To the left of that was the other tunnel. But it was dark. I hadn't left light on in the cave.

As I swam into the tunnel it quickly grew black and I had to feel my way along with my hands. It was fifty feet or so inside to the bottom of the cavern, but I couldn't see anything. It was so difficult now. I had to concentrate and wait until I reached a wall in front of me. Only then could I start up. But it seemed to take so long. That's always what happened when you were counting in seconds; it seemed to take forever.

When my hand hit rock in front of me I had to fight down a panic feeling. Something inside told me that the safest thing to do was to go back the way I had come, not go up into the dark unknown. For a second I hesitated. How much harder it was to think clearly at times like this. My instinct said, go back. My plan was to go forward. I had to force myself to trust the plan I had made before diving into the water. That was the hardest thing of all. If I were wrong, I wouldn't make it out. I wouldn't have enough air.

I went up steadily. Even as I did my mind fought against me, wanting to go back and save myself before it was too late. Was this suicide? I opened my eyes. Everything was black. Where was the surface? Why was the distance up so endless? Where was the surface? Where was the air? I needed air now!

When my hand struck a hard surface above me, panic went through me like an electric shock. My mouth opened and I swallowed water. It couldn't be. It couldn't be. I couldn't have made a mistake. Had I chosen the wrong cave? Was I about to die? My heart broke as I realized I was about to die.

In a split second I thought of Hollie and Seaweed. I thought of Ziegfried and Sheba. My grandparents. My father. My sister. I thought of Cinnamon and how sad she would be. I was so sorry. I was so sorry for all of them. I had let them down so terribly. In a final act of desperation I struck at the stone ceiling above me. It was strangely smooth. In a second I realized what it was. It was the sub. I swam desperately to the side, broke the surface and gasped for air, coughing and throwing up sea water. I clung to the side of the sub and cried. I had been frightened to death. It was the closest I had ever come to dying. I didn't like it one little bit.

But there was no time to waste. I climbed into the sub, hit the floodlights and went down and out through the tunnel. The undertow tugged at the sub as it came into the sea and it scraped and bumped against rock on the way up. As I approached the surface the waves tossed and pitched the sub wildly. I had several ropes ready to tie up to the rock if it were at all possible. I didn't mind a few scrapes, but I needed to keep it from getting bashed against the rocks.

I surfaced completely and opened the hatch. The wind almost blew me right out of the portal. I strapped on the harness and tied myself to the sub with a fifty-foot length of rope. I tied a rope to the dinghy and then inflated it on the side of the sub, jumped into it and paddled over to the rock. Water was spilling into the sub but I wasn't worried about that. It wouldn't swamp so quickly. I saw the hollow where Seaweed and Hollie were. I yelled but they couldn't hear me.

Reaching the rock, I climbed out and tied the dinghy down, but it wouldn't stay for long. I climbed up the rock and found the crew. Hollie was still inside the tool bag. He was such a smart dog. I sealed the hatch on the bag and swung it over my shoulder. Then I tried to pick up Seaweed but he would have none of that. "Follow me, Seaweed! Biscuits! Biscuits!" I had to yell it at the top of my lungs for him to hear me. I started down the rock. He started to follow by hopping but the wind picked him up. I flung myself at him, caught him in the air and pulled him against my chest. I knew he didn't like that, but too bad. When we reached the dinghy I shoved Seaweed inside my shirt. That was the only way I could hold on to him, untie the ropes and paddle to the sub. The second we climbed out of the dinghy the wind grabbed it, snapped the rope and ripped it away. I saw it fly away into the sky like a leaf. I climbed into the sub, let Seaweed out from under my shirt, shut the hatch, went down and submerged. It was a bumpy descent. We banged rock several times but I found the tunnel on sonar, motored into it and rose into the peace and quiet of the cavern. I didn't think anyone was ever so happy to be inside a cave before.

Chapter 31

THE TYPHOON RAGED. It was an act of nature. Paul said that the typhoons were getting worse every year because of global warming, which was our fault. He said we didn't deserve this planet. But then, he didn't believe he deserved his own freedom.

I fed the crew, made some pasta, cleaned myself up and tried to grab some sleep. I hoped Cinnamon was safe where she was. I hoped Paul was too. There was nothing I could do anyway until the typhoon passed. So I tried to sleep.

But I couldn't. I needed to know what was happening. A few hours after we had come in, I climbed through the passageways again, by myself, until I reached the last one. The echo of the winds twisted deeply inside, even before I slithered up the final section. It was much louder than before. I slithered up anyway and stuck my head out. The force of the typhoon was frightening. Would anyone survive this?

Back in the cavern I sat on the hull and stared at the skeletons. Who were they anyway, I wondered? What were their lives like before they joined the army and went to war? And why did they come here? Did they even have a choice about coming? Perhaps they didn't. Perhaps they never wanted to come here. Then they died here. They must have had family and friends waiting for them back home, wherever home was. But they never returned. They would have been listed as missing-in-action. Now, here we were, sitting in their tomb as if we had snuck in like ghosts. Well, we had. I honestly didn't know who seemed more like ghosts—us, or them.

Should I just leave them then, because this was their grave? I would have, I thought, if I knew they didn't have people waiting for them, wondering about them and what had happened to them. But there had to be people wondering still, such as the man on the cliffs, because everyone comes from somewhere. Everyone has people who want to know what happens to them.

Then I wondered: what if I had been one of them? Would I want people to know what had happened to me? That was easy to answer. Yes, I sure would. I would want someone to tell my grandparents, my father, and especially Ziegfried, Sheba and Angel. Even if fifty years had passed since I died?

Yes, absolutely, even if five hundred years had passed.

Well, that settled it—when the typhoon was over, I would carry the skeletons out.

But how could I get them outside without taking them into the sub? And I really didn't want to take them into the sub. That was my home. I didn't want skeletons in it, even for a little while. But the passageways were too narrow to carry skeletons through, especially the last part at the top, unless I carried them bone by bone, and there was no way I was going to do that. It was one thing to share a cave with them; it was another to carry them on my back like a sack of potatoes. I would have to take them into the sub, I guessed, like it or not.

A few hours later I climbed up again. The typhoon had lessened some but it would be getting dark soon. I decided to wait until first thing in the morning when the sun was up. I would pack a lunch, bring Hollie and leave Seaweed behind with a light on.

The next day, when Hollie and I crawled out, the air was almost as still outside as it was inside the cave. But I couldn't believe what we found. The typhoon had caused so much destruction the land was hardly recognizable. Trees had been pulled right out of the ground, roots and all, and thrown sideways. I couldn't even tell where the road was when we went down the hill. Then we found it. Parts of it were clear and parts covered in debris. I saw large fish, shells and lots of seaweed from the bottom of the sea. How could it have come here? A little farther along the road we came across a dead cow. Now I was really worried. What were we going to discover in town? What about Cinnamon, Paul and everyone else? A little farther I heard the distant sound of a chainsaw. Someone was alive. Someone had begun to clean up.

On the way to town I saw the first houses. Every concrete house was still standing, but nothing else. Homes made of wood and metal were flattened and their materials scattered widely. I saw a sink, toilet and bathtub in the middle of the road. Then I came upon a crew of men working to clear the road, and they would not let me go any farther. "We need your help here!" they said, and it was no use arguing with them. I put Hollie down where I could see him and started helping pull things off the road. Two men cut the trees and branches on the road and I helped throw the pieces to the side. Everything would be gathered up later. For now, it was just necessary to make the road passable. People had to be able to reach the hospital.

"Was anyone killed?" I asked.

"At least a thousand," one man answered. "Nobody knows for sure. Could be a lot more. It's worse on the south side."

"Do you know if the circus ship survived?"

The men shook their heads. "Sorry, son. Didn't see it. Don't know."

I worked with the crew all morning. It was killing me not knowing whether Cinnamon and Paul were okay or not.

Nobody I met had seen the ship. Finally, when they took a break for lunch, I grabbed Hollie and snuck away. I was sure there were other crews I could help later; I didn't have to stay with this one.

The town was not as badly damaged as I thought it would be. Everyone had boarded up their windows. Now they were open again. I went straight to the dock. There were sailboats lying on their sides far from the water. I saw the circus ship docked just where it had been, though it looked more beaten up than before. It was covered with clumps of seaweed, sand and tree branches, but it was still there. Everyone must have survived. I hurried on. I wanted to see if Paul was okay.

The road that led to Paul's house was impassable. I had to climb over and around trees, branches and debris. The beach wasn't any better. There were crews clearing the road but I avoided them because I didn't want anyone to stop me before I reached Paul's house.

The house was still standing but the butterflies were gone. The lemons and coconuts were gone, and the fat banana leaves were gone. It looked so bare. The dogs were there, in the back, but Paul wasn't. I went to the door and knocked. The dogs yipped, then recognized me and wagged their tails. But where was Paul? Had he been injured? Had he gone to the hospital? The hospital was on another road. I had seen a sign for it. So, I headed in that direction. Then I saw another crew clearing the road. And then I saw Paul. He had taken off his jacket and was carrying small armloads of debris to the piles. He was moving as slowly as a snail but he was help-ing. I saw him talking to the other men and smiling. I could hardly believe it. Then he saw me. "Alfred!"

"Hi, Paul."

"What a mess, hey?"

I nodded.

"Have you come to help too?"

He sounded happy.

"Yes, I have."

I put Hollie down and let him out of the bag. Then I joined Paul and the rest of the crew.

We worked until dark. It took all of that time to clear a section of road about an eighth of a mile long. It was hard work, and no one was getting paid, and yet everyone was happy. I found that inspiring. It made me think that clean-ing up the oceans wouldn't be so hard if the right people came together to do it.

I wondered if Paul considered his house arrest over now. After all, he had come to the circus, and now he was working away from his house. But I didn't want to ask him that yet. It didn't feel right. I did tell him about the caves and skeletons though, and what I was planning to do with them. Perhaps it would upset him to hear about it, I didn't know. It didn't seem to. He listened closely, asked me a few questions, and then offered to help. "I can speak a little Japanese."

"You can speak Japanese?"

"A little."

"Cool."

When it turned dark, we stopped working. Paul went home and I returned to the circus ship. I checked to make sure the hatch was shut on the tool bag before climbing on board. I found Cinnamon in Megara's cabin. She pulled me in, shut the door and hugged me tightly. "I'm so happy you are all right. Did you hide in your cave?"

I nodded. "Is everyone here okay?"

"Yes, but it was awful. We were afraid. We thought it was going to capsize the ship."

"Really?"

"It turned us sideways. It almost threw us upside-down. We banged against the dock and dented the side of the ship."

"But you're all right?"

"I'm fine. I'm better now that I know that you are okay."

I looked behind Cinnamon and saw Megara watching me. Even without her make-up and costume she looked like Medusa. I waved. "Hi."

"Hello, Alfred. You survived?"

"Yes. I had a safe place to stay."

"And you enjoyed our circus?"

I looked down. A snake was coiling around my ankle. Carefully, I lifted my foot free. "Uhh . . . yes. Very much. Where will you go next?"

"Nowhere for a while. We have to make repairs first. Our next venue will be Guam, I believe."

I felt a tap on my shoulder. It was another snake.

"They're getting used to you," said Megara.

I brushed the snake away.

"Do you want to take a walk?" Cinnamon asked.

"Sure."

Hollie and I were always happy to leave the snake lady's den.

We went slowly down the beach. The power was out on the island and wouldn't be up for at least a week. People were running generators. Cinnamon held my hand. She was happy. She hadn't heard of anyone being killed. I realized that the man who had told me that had been exaggerating a lot.

"Cinnamon?"

"Yes?"

"I want to ask you something."

"Okay."

"It's kind of weird, and I would understand if you didn't want to help, I really would."

"I would love to help. What is it?"

"It's . . . well, I'm going to take the skeletons out of the cave and I could use your help."

"You're right; that's weird."

"Paul is going to help too."

"You mean the crazy guy?"

"He's not crazy. Well, maybe he's a tiny bit crazy. But he's very nice. It's okay if you don't want to help. I understand. I just thought I'd ask you because you said you weren't made of glass."

"Will I have to look at the skeletons?"

"I suppose you could shut your eyes, but I think it would be very hard not to see them. They're not that scary. Honestly. Just a little."

"I think they're going to be very scary. Will I have to touch them?"

"I don't think you'd have to touch them, just the bags we would carry them in."

"What kind of bags?"

"I was thinking of using those large burlap sacks we have for the road clean-up."

"Oh boy, that's weird. Okay, I'll help."

"Really? That's great. Thanks."

"You're welcome. You live a crazy life."

"I know. So do you."

Chapter 32

FOR SIX DAYS PAUL and I worked with a clean-up crew. There was so much to do. All of the roads needed clearing. Ditches needed clearing so the water could run off the roads and fields. Wires had to be picked up and reconnected before power could be restored. People needed help cleaning their yards so they could get back to normal life. The official report said that twenty-seven people had died during the typhoon. Most had been struck by debris, drowned, or died of a heart attack.

I didn't see Cinnamon the second night because I had to return to the cave to feed Seaweed and let him out. The night after that I was so exhausted from work that I fell asleep on a cosy spot beside the road, just intending to nap, but didn't wake until the next morning. So it was three nights later when I finally came back to the ship. But I knew she would understand why I had not been around.

We walked each night after that. In the days, I worked out a plan with Paul. In the nights, I shared it with Cinnamon. Each night I slept on the beach with Hollie and Seaweed, and each morning washed in the lagoon. I had coffee and toast with Paul first thing every morning, and lunch and supper with the work crew. People brought us food and we picked up fruit during the day wherever we found it, so I was well fed. I felt like a hobo in a way, eating and sleeping outside all of the time, like Seaweed. And what a wonderful feeling it was.

The night we went for the skeletons, Cinnamon walked across the island with me. Twilight was passing when we reached the spot on the shore where Seaweed had hidden from the wind. Cinnamon waited with Hollie while I dove into the water. But she was struggling with it. "You are going to dive down there and come back with your submarine?"

"Yup."

"And then I'll come down there with you and we'll pick up the skeletons and bring them back?"

"Yup."

"Okay. For some reason I can't quite believe this."

"It's okay. You'll see. I'll be right back."

I did my breathing and dove into the sea. It was much easier without an undercurrent, and I felt a lot more confident that I was going in the right direction. Even so, it was unnerving to enter the blackness again and swim up into the cavern knowing that I *had* to be right, that a mistake would mean death. I thought of Mr. Chee again, as I knew I always would now at moments of danger. What would he have done in my shoes, I wondered?

I swam up inside the cavern, climbed into the sub and brought it down and out into the sea. When I rose to the surface and opened the hatch, it was completely dark. I could barely make out Cinnamon's silhouette on the rocks. We didn't have a dinghy anymore so I hit the floodlights and came to the edge of the rock. She passed me Hollie first, then the burlap sacks, then jumped onto the hull. We submerged and went into the cavern. I kept the floodlights on. Cinnamon was nervous when she stuck her head out of the portal. "Oh! Oh my gosh! Are those real?"

"Of course they're real."

"They don't look real."

"They are."

"I know, I know. They just don't look it. They look fake or something."

I brought the sub to touch the ledge, then we jumped over with the sacks. Cinnamon grew very quiet now. I asked her to hold open the sacks while I lifted each skeleton inside. She nodded and held open a sack. I picked up the head first and put it in the sack, because I knew it would fall off anyway. Cinnamon made a whimpering sound and squinted her eyes shut. I put the skull in as gently as I could, then picked up the rest of the skeleton by holding on to the uniform. It wasn't too hard, but a few bones slipped out.

"Please open the bag as wide as you can."

"Okay. Sorry."

I slid the skeleton in, picked up the extra bones, dropped them in, and then tied up the top tightly with a piece of twine. "Okay. That's one. That wasn't too bad."

Cinnamon shivered. "Please hurry!"

"Okay."

We bagged the other skeletons. Then we carried them one at a time into the sub and piled them inside the engine compartment, which was a tight squeeze. I took one last look at the cavern that had been our protection from the typhoon, and the soldiers' tomb. I was glad I had taken photographs already. I would never forget it anyway. We submerged and went out into the sea.

We sailed around the island and into the lagoon, surfacing under the bow of the circus ship. Paul was waiting on the dock with a cart. We carried the bags up the ladder of the dock one at a time and laid them on the cart. Paul looked distressed. I asked him if he was okay.

"I'm fine, Alfred. I really am. I am just so glad to be doing this. It is an honour for me. You cannot know what it means."

I nodded. I knew that was true.

When all of the skeletons were on the cart, Paul wrapped a blanket around them and tied it down. I went back to the sub and brought Hollie out. Then I took the sub down so that the portal was just a foot above the surface and tied it up to a rope ladder Cinnamon dropped on the other side of the ship. I swam back to the ladder and climbed onto the wharf.

"Now," said Paul, "I will push the cart to my house, and tomorrow I will call the police and explain what I found. And I will call the man who gave you his number, and we will find the identities of these men and contact their families."

"Thank you," I said.

"No, Alfred. Thank you. You have helped more than I can say. Will you promise to come back and visit me?"

"I will. I promise."

"He keeps his promises," Cinnamon said.

Paul reached out his hand. When I shook it I felt fresh blisters from the work on the road. I also felt strength in his hand I hadn't felt before. "I *will* come back," I said. I knew that I would.

He smiled, though it was a sad smile. He nodded to Cinnamon, turned and started pushing the cart slowly away. I felt my eyes water suddenly, and had to bite my lip.

"Are you okay?" Cinnamon asked.

"Yup. I'm just . . . tired, I guess."

In truth, there were no words to describe the sight of that old man walking away.

I stood and watched until he became nothing but a

shadow, then barely a shadow, and then nothing.

What did it all mean? What had it all been for? I didn't understand any of it. And maybe I never would.

We left Saipan in the middle of the night. Cinnamon and I took one final walk. She tried to talk me into staying longer, to join the circus for just a while, to see what it was like. I was tempted really, but I had so much more to do now, besides places to explore and things to discover. I wanted to learn more about the health of the sea, how to clean it up and protect it. This was my path now, just as the circus was hers. But I knew our paths would cross again. I just knew it. And I didn't need Sheba to tell me.

Epilogue

THE SEA ROLLED in silver and blue swells, as it would anywhere, except maybe the Arctic. But the air was hot, so very
hot, unlike anywhere else I had ever been. You wouldn't last
long in an open boat here, without shade or fresh water. You
would die of exposure perhaps almost as quickly as you
would die of exposure in the north Atlantic. That seemed
ironic to me. A lot of things about the Pacific seemed ironic.

But I had answers to some of my questions now. Were the
waves bigger in the Pacific? Yes, I thought so. Were the storms
bigger? Definitely. Was there something about places that
drew extraordinary events to happen there? There seemed
to be. That's what it felt like to me, and I would continue to
believe that, at least for now.

Was I sorry to have seen some of the darker things? Yes and no. But I was catching only a glimpse through a "glass darkly." I hadn't been here when the worst things had happened. I had seen the garbage for myself, yes, and the typhoons and shrimp trawlers, but I hadn't seen the suicides, people on fire, or the battles or nuclear explosions. I had seen only films of those things. And it wasn't the same. At least I wouldn't go through life not knowing those things had happened, or were happening somewhere else right now, some of them. I *wanted* to know what was happening in the world, good and bad, I really did. And I believed I could make a difference. It wasn't too late. We did deserve this planet. Hollie and Seaweed certainly deserved it. Ziegfried and Sheba deserved it. Cinnamon deserved it. The people cleaning up from the typhoon deserved it. Mr. Chee deserved it. Paul deserved it, even if he didn't think that he did. I believed that he did.

Three days from Saipan we picked up a weak signal on radar. It appeared and disappeared. I couldn't help getting my hopes up. Could it be Hugh? I wanted so much for it to be him, to see him again and know that he had survived all the terrible storms.

As we closed in on the signal I climbed the portal, strapped on the harness and scanned the water. I couldn't see anything. Perhaps it was just a floating can. And then, I saw the tiny splashes that a turtle's fins make. And I saw a spot on his back. But it wasn't Hugh. It was another turtle with a transmitter and a yellow spot. It didn't matter. I felt the same thrill. Of all the things I had seen in my life so far, none filled me with so much awe as the sight of a sea turtle swimming across the vast ocean all by itself. Sea turtles had been doing it for millions of years, long before humans ever took a step on the earth—swimming along like tireless, peaceful warriors. It filled me with awe.

I pulled alongside him to see if he would rest, as Hugh had rested. Then it occurred to me—perhaps this turtle wasn't a he, but a she. I tried to think of a good name for a girl and decided to call her Penelope. Seaweed promptly jumped onto her back. I carried Hollie out and let him look and sniff. The great turtle hugged the side of the sub and shut her eyes. We stayed and watched until we grew sleepy too. After a while, I went to bed. As I lay on my cot and felt the hot Pacific air drift into the sub, carrying the faint scent of burning, I thought of Ziegfried and Sheba, and how much I missed them. And very slowly I drifted off to sleep.

When I woke, the turtle was gone.

Standing in the portal with Hollie, while Seaweed flew above us, I read a few lines from *The Rime of the Ancient Mariner* in the sea turtle's honour.

> *Farewell, farewell! but this I tell*
> *To thee, thou Wedding-Guest!*
> *He prayeth well, who loveth well*
> *Both man and bird and beast.*

ABOUT THE AUTHOR

Philip Roy continues to live and write in Nova Scotia. Whenever possible, he travels to the places he writes about in the Submarine Outlaw series. From 1999 to 2001, he lived on the island of Saipan, which features in *Ghosts of the Pacific*. Recently he travelled to India to research the fifth book in the series, to be released in 2012. His next journey will be to Mozambique and South Africa. Travelling makes for great adventure, Philip contends. The only thing better is writing about it and visiting schools to share his stories with young readers.